An
Early
Hairst

Bob
Mitchell

An Early Hairst

Bob Mitchell

Published in 2008 by YouWriteOn.com

Copyright Text Bob Mitchell

First Edition

Published by YouwriteOn.com

Bob Mitchell

Bob was born and brought up on an Aberdeenshire croft bearing a remarkable similarity to the "Mossyhillock" of this tale.

He trained as a psychiatric nurse in the late 1960s and spent most of his career in Nurse Education.

He retired from his position of Senior Lecturer, (Mental Health) at Napier University, Edinburgh in 2002.

Bob retains a keen interest in many aspects of community life and is a Justice of the Peace in the Lothian and Borders Sheriffdom.

He is a keen admirer of our National Bard Robert Burns and is an active speaker in Burns circles.

He is currently involved in an ambitious project to restore three historical sites relating to the Burns family in East Lothian and has appeared in Burns related events in the Edinburgh Festival Fringe.

He is a lifelong, enthusiastic, and unrepentant supporter of Aberdeen Football Club.

He has lived in Haddington, East Lothian since 1973.

He has a wife, Anne, three grown up "children" and two adorable grandchildren, James and Sophie. Lucy, a West Highland Terrier, completes his family.

Shada

Shada, the canine heroine of the tale was originally called Scruffy and the author developed a clear picture of her in his mind's eye.

On completion of his manuscript and while visiting a hill top farmstead in Cuba, he was enthusiastically welcomed by a local dog who looked identical to Scruffy in every way.

She was called Sombra, the Spanish word for Shadow and after a quick translation into the Doric, Shada was born.

The author wishes her and her human companions in Cuba all that they could wish themselves.

Acknowledgements

The Photos appearing on the covers of this publication appear on
www.scran.ac.uk and are reproduced with their kind permission.

The author has quoted significantly from the works of several poets
and songwriters and is happy to acknowledge his grateful thanks for
their input.

These include: The Burial of Sir John Moore after Corunna: Charles
Wolfe (1791 – 1823)

The Charge of the Light Brigade; Alfred, Lord Tennyson (1809 –
1902)

Requiem; Robert Louis Stevenson (1850 – 1894)

The Tay Bridge Disaster; William McGonagall (1825 – 1902)

Pretty Little Black Eyed Susie; Kathleen Twomey, Fred Wise,
Benjamin Weisman

Living Doll; Lionel Bart

In addition he is pleased to acknowledge the contributions
during the writing and publishing of this book of:
Anne Mitchell, Ella Moir and
David Murray.

Many thanks to YouWriteOn.com and the Arts Council, England
for facilitating the publishing process

<u>CONTENTS</u>

Front Cover, (top to bottom) A North East Landscape, Turning Hay

Leith Walk (All circa 1959)

Aa Diffrint Noo

Granda, fit is hyowin neeps?
Fits leadin hame the stooks?
Fit di the mean b' coalin hey?
I canna fin't in books

Yir richt ti ask me that, ma loon
Cis me, an' fitsizname,
Fifty 'eers ago n' mair
Its fit we did at hame.

Bob Mitchell 2008

First appeared in "Fit Like Yer Majesty" published by Reading
Bus Press 2008

9

One More River

David stretched forward in his seat, desperately trying to spot the distinctive red structure. Just half an hour after saying farewell to his mother, here he was about to eye what he genuinely believed to be one of the wonders of the modern world. It was 1959 and he had already seen artists' impressions of the proposed road bridge over the Firth of Forth, but that unlikely venture was in the future: right now, the Forth Rail Bridge, the longest cantilever bridge in the world, reigned supreme.

The massive feat of engineering was well known to David. For others it joined the Lothians with the "Kingdom" of Fife, but for him it marked the dividing line, as distinctively as any customs post could, between the austere but familiar everyday living in post war Edinburgh and the equally impoverished and time warped parish of Balcrannie somewhere north of Aberdeen. This was the land of his forefathers, where his granny and granda still eked out a living in their tiny croft and where David had spent every summer holiday he could remember.

But this time he was on his own.

David had been twelve for some two months, and old enough, his mother reasoned to make the familiar journey unaccompanied. Unaccompanied, that was, except for an enormous list of instructions and the reassurance that he would be met at the Joint Station, Aberdeen, by a familiar face.

Bringing up David, largely on her own, had not been easy for Peggy Gordon, but she was becoming increasingly certain that, this slightly introverted young individual who had turned her world so upside down a few years ago, was going to turn out fine. The balancing act of being a lone parent and the demands of her long shifts at Craighouse Asylum was bearing fruit. He was going to be okay.

David peered across at the grimy looking character diagonally across the compartment from him and decided that he was still sleeping off the excesses of the night before. He had seen his likes many times before in Leith Walk and he held no fear of them. The only other occupants of the carriage were a young awkward looking mother and her scrawny baby. Her eyes were pointedly averted, as she stared with grim determination at the passing countryside. Her message was clear; she did not wish to engage in small talk.

David was delighted, he was alone with his thoughts and last week's "Wizard" that he had begged off Tony Togneri when he came to wish him good luck, the night before.

But now was not the time to read. The train was chugging determinedly towards the bridge and soon he would actually be on it, perched like a miniscule model, seemingly miles above the water. 'It was the only place for twenty miles around,' the wags liked to say, 'where you could not see the Forth Bridge!'

He ran out of the compartment and into the corridor, clutching the silver sixpence, with which he could ill afford to part, but rituals were important for David. Ever since he could remember, his mother had given him a penny at this point in the journey and David had desperately tried to throw it into the river and thus assure himself good fortune. As far as he could recall, he had never quite made it, and apart from one memorable occasion when he had almost struck an unfortunate linesman, his pennies had invariably landed on the track, usually inches from where his open window had been.

To make matters worse, Tony had last night assured him that only silver coins worked, and with silver three-penny bits being almost obsolete, his potential filled sixpence had to be sacrificed.

The result was much as before, the sixpence bouncing once before coming to rest at the side of the track, leaving David to ponder on the futility of superstition and to wonder if the aforementioned linesman, went home at night with his pockets bulging.

Fife, and the even longer Tay Bridge beckoned and David knew that despite himself, he would experience an involuntary shiver as he looked down to the still visible remains of the original bridge, destroyed one winter's night almost eighty years before along with the Edinburgh train and its unfortunate passengers.

The much-ridiculed words of the 'poet' McGonagall sprang to mind:

Beautiful Railway Bridge of the Silv'ry Tay!
Alas! I am very sorry to say
That ninety lives have been taken away
On the last Sabbath day of 1879,
Which will be remembere'd for a very long time.

How David and his mum had laughed when they first read the words of McGonagall, like himself a native of Edinburgh, although usually associated with Dundee, and yet, some people claimed he was Scotland's second best known poet. Second only to Robert Burns whose two hundredth anniversary had been marked with a special issue of postage stamps in Russia earlier in the year.

It was time to put all thoughts of poetry and the still distant Tay behind him, and to settle down with "The Wizard".

Although hardly an approved work of literature, David was secretly rather proud that he had graduated to reading "The Wizard".

Unlike "The Dandy" and "The Beano" of his earlier years, "The Wizard" was not full of large pictures of unusual characters whose speech was contained in balloons and seemed usually to consist of "eeks' and "ughs" and similar utterances guaranteed to drive parents and teachers insane. And yet, David knew his mother read them from cover to cover and even Miss Playfair, in what must have been unguarded moments, had been heard to mention "Desperate Dan" and "Dennis the Menace"!

But "The Wizard" was altogether more grown up, as befitted his status as a Primary Seven pupil. The print was

13

small and closely packed together. Pictures were usually confined to the top of the first page of each story and some of the many advertisements.

David's heroes consisted of regulars like "Wilson", the athlete with a secret and a fondness for herbal concoctions and "Alf Tupper" the motor cycle driving plumber turned runner who trained on fish suppers! These were augmented with a fairly generous helping of war stories, invariably set in the Second World War, demonstrating the grit of the British Army and its ability to get out of all scrapes by the foot of the final page.

The adverts were of genuine interest to David, particularly since he had learned that they provided the bulk of all newspapers and comics' income. He felt vaguely disappointed that his coppers meant so little to the publishers, but was delighted with many of the advertisements on which they apparently depended.

Prominent among these were colourful accounts about life in the armed forces, aimed at recruiting what was usually called "boy soldiers" from the age of sixteen. Life in the army certainly seemed attractive to David, consisting, as it appeared of sport, travel and the opportunity to choose from an unbelievable amount of trades and occupations.

David knew that he would eventually end up in the forces. National Service meant that every boy was called up for two years when they reached the age of eighteen and the thought left him strangely unmoved. He had already decided that he would plump for the Army, they needed most recruits, and those requesting the Navy or Air Force were often disappointed, anyway. More crucially, he had decided he wanted to be a "proper soldier" with a gun and a bayonet. He could be an electrician in Edinburgh. If he was going to the far-flung corners of the earth, he was going as a fighting machine, not a filing clerk.

He could just hear his mother's response to that suggestion and decided he wouldn't mention it just yet. His father, he understood had been killed in the war, clearly making life difficult for him and his mum. Strangely, he knew little about his dad, and had never thought to ask. He rather liked there being just the two of them in that two roomed, second floor flat, but one day he would need to know a bit more. But that, he decided could wait.

David grimaced at the "Charles Atlas" advert, which boasted 'You too can have a body like mine!' and depicted a muscle man of unlikely proportions promising to change the lives of all who sent for his free brochure.

After months of secret deliberations and nocturnal readings of the comic strip advert showing a former "seven stone weakling" coming to grips with a bully and winning the affections of a beautiful girl, David had decided to apply for the free brochure. He was only vaguely aware of what he might get up to with the beautiful girl, but it seemed infinitely better than having sand kicked in his face. A new life beckoned!

David cringed with embarrassment and he felt sure turned red as he recalled the day the envelope arrived, addressed to Mr D Gordon and marked "Private and Confidential". The brochure was free, but the course designed round something called "Dynamic Tension" cost eleven guineas; more than he could get his hands on in two years! Worse, he recalled was to follow. The original free brochure was the first of countless envelopes marked "Private and Confidential" that arrived for Mr D Gordon with ever more lavish promises of the body beautiful if only he parted with his money.

For reasons unknown, the postman, himself a "seven stone weakling" was obviously aware of the contents of the "Private and Confidential" envelopes and took to smirking or adopting "Mr Universe" type poses, when they met on the common stairwell leading to the flat. As if that was not bad enough he started calling him "Wee Geordie" after the hero of the popular film of a few years previously who had gone on to win Olympic Gold after applying to just such an advert.

The difference between fiction and fact, decided David, was immense!

The change in the engine noise and a sensation of slowing down, confirmed that the Tay Bridge was upon them, ghostly remains and all. Dundee, the destination of the mother and baby beckoned, the half way stage on his journey had been reached.

The second half of his journey would follow the coast northwards with the sea seldom disappearing from sight for more than a few minutes. It would also take longer. After a fairly quick journey through Fife the train was scheduled to stop at a number of coastal resorts before terminating in Aberdeen. Thereafter there was the bus.

Mossyhillock was a small croft of mediocre agricultural land and some ten-acre of adjoining moorland. It was part of a small estate consisting of "the big house", the home farm, and a number of lesser farms and crofts of which it was by far the smallest. It lay in a remote part of the parish of Balcrannie some twelve miles from the outskirts of Aberdeen. It had none of the modern facilities that even David, who lived in a poorer part of Edinburgh, took for granted and a summer of paraffin lamps and toilets in the garden awaited him. Yet no one seemed to complain.

A summer spent at Mossyhillock had many attractions, however, the foremost of which, were his grandparents Davy and Elsie Gordon, his granda and granny.

David hungrily tore into the sandwiches that his mother had made for him as day was breaking, ignoring her advice to chew carefully and eat his crusts. The crusts were quickly despatched from the same window as his sixpence had been thrown earlier and had been eagerly snapped up by one of a number of circling gulls.

The landscape was changing subtly and the soil in the large and fertile looking fields was becoming uniquely red in colour, telling David he was in the Mearns and heading for the county of Kincardine.

He thought back to the tiny living room of his home, the room in which his mother also slept, in the bed-sized alcove, which was usually hidden by large curtains.

16

His mother's passion was books, which all but covered the floor of their living room and took up every inch of space on the inexpertly erected shelves on two of the walls. And he thought of one of her favourites.

"Sunset Song", he knew was all about the folks of the countryside through which he was now passing. Folks not unlike his grandparents and their neighbours who had been tied to the land for hundreds of years and whose very staying alive depended on what little could be produced from the harsh and uncooperative landscapes that were their home.

The author, Lewis Grassick Gibbons, like David's mum, Peggy, had left the North East to make his living, he in the forces and in journalism, she to nurse in Edinburgh. Yet many had chosen to remain with the only life they knew.

David had already tried more than once to read "Sunset Song" but had found it hard going. The characters in Gibbons book seemed to speak in a language that he did not understand and which was neither working class Edinburgh, the North East Doric or the received pronunciation of the classroom all of which were familiar to him. His mum, however, did clearly not share his misgivings and David noticed that it was the one book to which she returned, possibly once a year, and which she re-read in the course of a few evenings.

David had been staring nervously for some time at the rugged coastline, willing himself to see Dunnotar Castle, which reassuringly promised that Stonehaven was fast approaching.

Stonehaven was a beautiful coastal town with its own harbour and open-air swimming pool. It was the last stop before Aberdeen.

Soon, it had come and gone and this was the spot, fifteen miles from their destination that Peggy invariably stood up and started collecting their bits and pieces with a view to disembarking. This preplanning had secretly embarrassed David for almost all of his short life. All around them others sat still, dosing or reading their papers whilst Peggy hurried and scurried, marking them both out, he was sure, as country bumpkins or inexperienced travellers. This was both untrue and unkind.

But this time was different. Now that he was on his own, 'Stonehaven,' he reasoned, 'seemed just about right.' Within five minutes, he was pressed against the exit door. Most of his worldly goods it seemed were crammed in his ex gas mask bag and a similar khaki coloured rucksack bought from the Army Surplus Store at the top of Leith Walk. His "Wizard" was crammed in the rear pocket of the short trousers, which he planned to discard forever as soon as he arrived. He was still ten miles from Aberdeen!

'Davy! Ma wee loon!' The whole of the Joint Station seemed to have gone momentarily and embarrassingly quiet as the owner of the foghorn voice, who was only vaguely familiar to David attempted to grab him in a massive bear hug.

'Dinna say that yi' dinna ken me,' boomed the voice. 'I'm Muggie, Muggie Burnett, the nurse. I trained wi' yir mither. I'm the district nurse at Polknappie, noo!'

David did indeed remember the nurse now, although as far as he could recall she had never been particularly friendly with his mother and looked about ten years older.

'I telt yir grunny that I wid see yi onto the bus at Mealmarket Street. Och, hurry up min, yir nae in Edinburgh noo. If yi hurry up we'll hae time for a cup o' tea and a buttery in the Princess Café afore the bus comes. Min it's a peety that yi hidnae come the morn.'

David cringed. 'If by any chance he might have been greeted by a more familiar face, tomorrow,' he reasoned, 'it was indeed a pity that he hadn't postponed his trip for a day.' Still, the prospect of a buttery, that unique northeast roll, lifted his spirits.

As he exited the station, two grey backed gulls swooped overhead and he inhaled a distinct smell of fish. His holidays had begun.

- 2 -

The Long and Winding Road

The short walk, from the station to the Princess Café, gave David time to ponder on his disappointment that it had been Nurse Burnet that had met him. After all, this was the first time he had made the journey on his own and despite her enthusiastic greeting, she was virtually a stranger to him. To make matters worse, she was a noisy stranger!

'Dinna sit there looking at yir buttery, loon,' she muttered. 'The bus leaves at twinty past five, and we've got another mile ti walk till Mealmarket Street.'

'Nearer half a mile' thought David, as he rehearsed the short walk in his mind, 'along part of two of Aberdeen's best known streets, Union Street and King Street.'

His mood changed immediately as Nurse Burnet yet again interrupted his reverie. 'Sandy Stronach winna sit and wait for yi, if yi dinna get there on time!'

Sandy Stronach was still driving the local bus! That was much better! Sandy, although probably as old as Peggy, was a great pal, and despite the demands of his timetable, David knew he would gladly have held up the bus for him had he known he was coming. Sandy looked at his timetable infrequently and stuck to it only loosely, but that's how he had always worked.

Several years ago, when David had asked his grandfather why the war in Europe had stopped several months before the one in Japan, old Davy had explained, 'It wisna planned that wye, but Sandy Stronach wis fighting in the Far East. Hiv yi iver kent Sandy ti be on time?'

Their destination reached, Maggie Burnet had slipped away, muttering something about seeing him tomorrow, although that seemed decidedly unlikely. David realised that she had gone before he could thank her and wondered briefly if he could have been a little friendlier. Then he didn't think about her again.

'Afteeernooon Colonaal Suuuur!' Bellowed, Sandy Stronach, clicking his heels and standing to attention with a mock salute as soon as he set eyes on David.

Two Mealmarket street pigeons that had been minding their own business hopped for cover.

'Foo are yi deein', loon?' he chortled, rapidly changing his posture to affectionately thump David on the back with his permanently gloved right hand. 'Dinna tell me I hiv ti pit up wi' you a' Simmer!'

'Colonel' had been Sandy's pet name for David for the last two or three years, ever since he had inadvertently let slip that his Edinburgh pals had taken to calling him "Colonel Nasser". This nickname had come about during the Suez crisis of 1956, when someone had thought David resembled the Egyptian dictator. His classmates had dropped it shortly afterwards, but when something tickled Sandy Stronach's fancy, he didn't let go.

Sandy had changed little in the past year although perhaps his hair had thinned a little while his ample tummy had done quite the opposite.

'Six stones,' Peggy had once confided, 'when he came home. And that was after they fattened him up.'

David mused that he must be nearer three times that weight now, and as Sandy again adopted the saluting pose to welcome him aboard, he seemed every inch the carefree clown.

The bus, painted in the green and yellow of the local company, that was now one of the few to have resisted being taken over by a large national concern, had room for thirty-five passengers, but was almost empty. It sported an ungainly device with a huge handle which had clearly been made by the local blacksmith and which allowed Sandy to operate the door from his seat.

'Meet my new clippie,' he joked, and for the first time David realised that Sandy was on his own. The conductress or "clippie," Lucy Walker, who had worked on the route for as

20

long as David could remember, had been sacked as a cost saving exercise. 'Broke her hert, it did,' confided Sandy. 'She's hardly been oot o' the hoose since'.

David sat in the front seat. Above him was a sign, which stated:

**Passengers Must Not Speak
To the Driver While the
Bus is in Motion**

Sandy pulled his handle, causing the door to rumble shut. He edged the bus onto the street and joined the traffic. 'Come on 'an, Colonel.' he grinned, 'Gi'es yir news!'

As the bus trundled down King Street towards the open road, David was only half an hour from Mossyhillock and for the first time since leaving Edinburgh he realised how much he wanted to see his grandparents again.

Far from giving Sandy his "news," it was David who wanted the answers. 'Had Sandy seen either of his grandparents recently? Had Granny taken the bus to Aberdeen? Had he met Granda when they were out with their dogs?'

David's mind flitted again. They were approaching the junction of King Street and Merkland Road East. Pittodrie Park, the home of Aberdeen Football Club was only a few hundred yards away!

David could not quite remember when he had decided to support Aberdeen Football Club in preference to either of the Edinburgh teams but it had cost him dear in arguments with his schoolmates. Hibs may play their home games only yards from his flat, but that was irrelevant. Football was a family thing and his family supported Aberdeen.

Sandy had no interest in football and therefore did not appreciate David's excitement at passing the stadium, but this part of town was significant to him as well.

'420 King Street,' he beckoned, 'that's where *my* granny lived. A great big gairden for us loons to play in.'

21

The stadium flashed past, and David felt momentarily envious of the old woman and her grandsons.

'Yi' winna, ken the brig noo,' Sandy smiled. And he was right!

As the bus crawled towards the bridge over the river Don and into the suburb that bore its name, David was once again reminded of the wonders of modern science. The bridge, always a traffic bottleneck, had doubled in width since David's last visit! The splendid new bridge had been opened by Her Majesty Queen Elisabeth only two months previously and seemed certain to allow unfettered access between town and county well into the next century.

The Don, as a river could scarcely match the scale and grandeur of the Forth or the Tay or the industrial might of the Clyde on the west coast, but along with its neighbour, the Dee, in the south, it neatly encapsulated the city and marked the beginning of the countryside.

The Bridge of Don was a rapidly expanding village, and although it enjoyed many of the modern conveniences of the city, it was decidedly in the country. To David's right, sprawled the large Army Barracks that was the home of the Gordon Highlanders, where many young national servicemen rapidly learned that the adverts in "The Wizard" and such like had been sparing with the truth.

To his left and on the top of a hill stood Bridge of Don School to where all the secondary schoolchildren from the parish of Balcrannie were transported daily. Helen, his inseparable holiday friend would have been attending there for the past year.

As if reading David's mind, Sandy broke the silence. 'Yi'll hardly ken that pal o' yours, noo.' he suggested with what David thought was a certain lack of approval. 'Quite the lady she's turned oot, and determined ti mairy that Elvis Presley, I understand.'

From the little he knew of Mr Presley, David understood that many people wanted to marry him; a large number of them from Edinburgh alone, so it seemed Helen might be doomed to disappointment. Nevertheless, he felt fleetingly alarmed. He realised now how eager he was to see Helen again, but how would she feel? He was desperately aware of his short trousers and lack of inches compared to most of his classmates. Surely that would make no difference to Helen and him?

They were now in the country and on the only bit of dual carriageway that David had ever seen. Sandy, like everyone else up there seemed to prefer to call it "the double road" and the concept seemed fascinating.

'Aye, Colonel,' he enthused, 'there may only be three mile o' it jist noo, but mark my words, the time will come fin there'll be double road a' the wye between Aiberdeen and Edinburgh.'

David stifled a laugh. Part of Sandy's charm was his enthusiasm, but his judgement was sometimes way wide of the mark. It was much more likely, he decided that Helen Sutherland would marry Elvis Presley!

The roads quickly narrowed and the bus slowly edged towards the village of Polknappie, if indeed it could be called a village. In reality, it consisted of about four "original" houses, which may have been about one hundred years old, and a shop of roughly the same age. Close by, had been added the nurse's house, now occupied by Maggie Burnet, and eight modern houses built, perhaps, at the end of the war. A good half mile further on, were the two other amenities, a church that opened once a month, and a two roomed primary school. The lay out of the village meant everyone had to walk for everything: some further than others.

The bus was now chugging uphill towards Balcrannie on quite the narrowest road David had ever seen. Low growing branches on the many trees fluttered gently in the breeze and came within inches of striking the bus. On the odd occasion when the company rather foolishly put a double decker on the route, the branches would loudly smash against the front upstairs window, causing customers of a timid disposition to duck nervously and those a few seats back to guffaw somewhat unconvincingly. David had never heard of a window being broken or anyone being hurt on such occasions.

'It micht as well be Blackpool!' Sandy moaned, pointing disapprovingly at the twenty-four houses and solitary phone box that made up the village of Balcrannie. David struggled unsuccessfully to spot the similarity.

'They've got the electric in!' Sandy explained, 'half o' them even burn lichts in mair than one windae at a time. Yi widnae get that wi the paraffin lumps.' The phone box seemed to radiate a beam worthy of any lighthouse. 'Some o' them hiv even got television!'

'Television!' David's ears pricked up. He had had a television for as long as he could remember and the lack of such a facility in Mossyhillock had always been the major down side of his holidays there. 'Now' he convinced himself, 'if he could have all the fun he associated with Mossyhillock *and* see a few of his favourite programmes, this could be the holiday of a lifetime.'

He was almost there. Soon they would be approaching the road end where David would get off and only a mile long country lane would separate David and his grandparents.

David was silently bemoaning the fact that the road had no name and was more than delighted that Sandy knew without being asked where to offload him. It could be highly embarrassing to have to explain to a strange driver or conductor where you were going, when in fact, it was literally nowhere.

It was then that David saw the notice for the first time. It was quite different from the usual notices on buses, warning the occupants to avoid spitting, smoking or standing beyond a certain point. It was hand made and proudly announced:

Burma Star Association

Grand Dance and Prize Raffle
with
Wattie Law

Victoria Hall
Balcrannie

Friday, 14th August   8 p.m.

2s 6d

A Stronach, Secretary.

'A Stronach. Is that you, Sandy? Are you a secretary? What's the Burma Star Association? Why are they having a dance?'

They had reached the road end.

'Come on Colonel,' he said, the twinkle momentarily gone from his eye. 'Yir grandfather's waiting. I'll be seein' yi.'

- 3 -

A Safe Haven

David had not expected to be met at the road end and certainly did not expect what happened next.

His grandfather, slightly older looking, but beaming from ear to ear, was clambering off what David recognised to be an ancient tractor.

'Welcome, laddie!' he chortled. 'Meet Fergie, my -' he hesitated. 'Fergie!'

David recognised that the ancient vehicle was indeed a Ferguson, the grey coloured tractor ideally suited for smaller farms.

'Jump on,' he indicated, although to where he should jump, David was uncertain.

The tractor was clearly built for one, but old Davy had thought of that, and a sack previously used to carry potatoes was folded several times to make a temporary, passenger "seat".

With a whoop of excitement, Davy crunched the gear stick forward, and the engine spluttered alive. The tractor lunged forward, on what David realised was the middle of the road. The speed seemed much faster than the twenty miles per hour or so which in reality, it was travelling, and David held on tight!

Granda had never passed a driving test, nor did it seem likely that he ever would; yet strangely he possessed a full driving licence! Before some date in the distant past, tests had not existed and people of his granda's vintage merely applied for a licence and took to the road. 'Not a good idea!' thought David!

The journey was short and by necessity, lacking in conversation, with David sitting back-to-back with his grandfather and staring nervously from whence he came.

The full, horrible implication of what his grandfather's purchase of the tractor might mean had no sooner entered

26

David's head than it was immediately dispelled! As the machine gurgled to a slightly premature stop an unmistakably whinnying noise could be heard from the direction of the corn yard.

Tibbie, the last, ancient, working Clydesdale horse in the parish, was a foal again, as she cantered towards her beloved pal. David rushed to meet her, tears suddenly appearing from nowhere as he grabbed her in an embrace. The long months since their last meeting had disappeared as Tibbie searched for the sugar lump that had travelled half the length of Scotland.

Tractors cannot look peevish, which is just as well, because old Fergie would have been completely brassed off!

With a quick promise to meet at first light, boy and beast parted company. David ran towards the ramshackle crofter's house and an eagerly awaited reunion with his grandmother, while Tibbie dragged her arthriticy bones to the shelter of the corn ricks.

As usual, Granny's welcome was as understated as it was sincere. No enthusiastic bear hugs or flamboyant kisses. 'Hullo, David.' She said simply. 'It's afa fine tae see yi.'

The house was a simple two bed roomed affair with a lean to "milk house" that was in fact a large pantry that had been converted into an additional bedroom. For years this room had been known as "Ted's room," after the uncle he had never met, but this was where David slept, and slowly it was becoming "David's room."

It was hard for David to realise that Uncle Ted actually existed, although undoubtedly he did. Like so many young men of his generation, Ted had been "called up" to fight the Nazi menace, but unlike many of his pals, he had apparently survived unscathed. According to Peggy, her big brother was now in India, but his name never seemed to crop up in any conversations that David overheard.

This suited David, as he had no desire to share his rather splendid little room with some uncle whose authenticity could not be verified. The room had a door that lead directly outside, and with his grandparents both being sound sleepers, it had allowed many sugary midnight feasts to take place between David and the ever hungry Tibbie.

The rest of the house consisted of a living room with an open fire on which all of the cooking took place and which doubled as a dining room. This room was somewhat confusedly, always called the kitchen and was the one room that was ever heated.

Attached to the front of the house was a wooden porch that had seen better days. It contained a hand pump from which all the water was obtained and a large sink that drained into a bucket directly beneath it. The toilet was at the end of the garden path.

'Can I go for a walk, Granny?' David asked as he drained the glass of milk that had greeted him on his arrival. After all it wasn't eight o'clock yet and the summer evenings up here seemed to stretch forever.

To his surprise, his grandmother started as if she had been asleep, but then smiled. 'On you go,' she said. 'Take care.'

David had a lot of catching up to do with his granny, but he had six weeks in which to do it. Six weeks in which he would never experience the sights and sounds of Auld Reekie or gaze wistfully at the London Road which started practically at his front door.

'Some day,' he thought.

At a whistle from David, Shada, a dark coloured, shaggy coated mongrel appeared from beneath the table, pausing to sniff at his legs with a show of reluctance. Her name meant "Shadow" in the North East vernacular and for the next six weeks the half collie, half terrier would be just that: David's constant companion. It was her invariable custom, however, to give him a muted welcome. Clearly she did not appreciate his habit of disappearing for months at a time and felt that at least momentarily; he should be made to suffer.

Point made, the two of them bounded towards the cart track and the moss as the rough moorland, which gave the croft, its name was invariably called.

The moss was where old Davy and many of the local men dug peat in a way that had changed little for hundreds of years. The peat was cut from the soil in a rectangular, flattened brick shape and in a moist to wet condition. After several weeks drying in the unpredictable sunlight they would be carted home and built into a large stack right next to the house where they would be used to supply the winter's warmth. Apart from the firewood from an occasional storm damaged tree, David never saw any other fuel burned in the croft house.

David expected that he would help his granda with the peats during the next few weeks, and if previous years were anything to go by there would also be hay to make, if only the sun would shine. The harvest proper, invariably called "the hairst," when the oats would be cut and "stooked" to dry, before being "led" back to the cornyard to await the threshing machine, would take place after David was safely back in Edinburgh.

Unknown to David, his grandfather was looking forward to his contribution this year, as never before. In the past he had enjoyed indulging his grandson's attempts at helping without ever expecting to see any end product. Now, he hoped David would be able to relieve him of some of what seemed to be an ever-increasing burden.

The "pirate ship" silhouetted the skyline as it had done for many years now, menacing and sinister and some three miles from the sea!

In reality, the "pirate ship" was a Douglas fir, partially uprooted by a storm of some years ago and bearing, to David's fertile imagination, a remarkable similarity to a large sailing vessel of years gone by. The ample branches were easy to climb, and David had long since mastered the easiest way to reach the top in a few short minutes. There he was rewarded by a real live "crows nest" just like in the best storybooks. However, this was no look out platform on which hapless crewmembers scanned the ocean main, but rather the home of a solitary or "hoodie" crow that raised a family there every year. David loved this play on words, and secretly scorned the

29

less imaginative locals who were somewhat unsure exactly what they might find amidst the topmost branches.

Yet others gradually succumbed to his fantasies and there was neither a farm servant nor a child for miles around who did not now call the old tree, the "pirate ship".

Nothing had changed. Shada patiently sat at the foot of the tree, while David, proving he had lost none of his agility, swung upwards, from branch to branch. Although, the light was beginning to fade, the view was as stunning as ever and despite lacerating his knee for what would be the first of many times that summer, David felt exhilarated. He had survived the journey north, renewed a couple of friendships and was beginning to feel entirely at home. Nothing had changed.

'Fifteen men and a dead man's chest
Yo ho ho and a bottle of rum'

He hollered to the empty moorland, in what he considered to be an authentic pirate acclaim! Then suddenly, he was a parrot! 'Pieces of eight!' he shrieked in his best bird voice, 'Pieces of eight!'

It was then that he realised that he was not alone! Someone was watching him from the shelter of the evergreen foliage at the foot of the spreading tree. Someone so familiar that Shada felt no need to investigate or growl a half-hearted warning.

'Well, well,' she grinned, clearly enjoying the moment. 'I thocht yi wid turn up, David.'

It was Helen and she *had* changed

- 4 -

Laying Plans

David was uncertain as to when he had first thought of his plan, but he had thought of little else for several weeks now. As he finished his boiled egg on that first holiday breakfast, he decided to tackle Granny about it right away. After all, the project, as he understood it would take a month to complete, so there was little time to waste.

'Granny,' he ventured, 'do you think it would be possible for me to hatch out some ducklings, this summer? After all, its two years since the last of the old ones disappeared.'

Granny looked ready to dismiss the idea out of hand. 'Dukes dinna pey.' She said uncertainly.

David knew that there was no economic argument for raising ducks in such a small scale, but was ready with his reply. 'But we all like dukes' eggs,' he reasoned triumphantly!

He smiled inwardly at his use of the north eastern word "duke" instead of "duck". The regal sounding name he felt was entirely appropriate for the majesty with which these birds graced the water, but he felt guilty that he could never think of the Queen's husband without imagining him bottom up in a millpond!

As an only grandchild and being the possessor of a winning smile, David usually managed to get his way eventually, but he was surprised at the speed of his granny's capitulation. A distant twinkle in her eye suggested that she might actually be looking forward to the idea.

'Well,' she announced, 'if we're gaun tae dae it we're gaun tae dae it richt. And the first thing we need is a hen!'

David was exasperated. Why didn't old people, even his own grandmother, ever listen to him? It was ducklings he wanted, not chickens.

31

But David had much to learn about country ways, and the first thing they needed was indeed a hen; a broody hen that would be prepared to sit on its clutch of eggs for twenty eight days. Ducks, it appeared are less reliable mothers and may abandon the eggs before they hatch or fail to keep them adequately warm to incubate them. Hens are much better.

David discovered that not any hen would do but only one that was broody or as Granny called it "cloackin'." Such hens would stop laying and as part of their regular cycle, would prepare themselves to sit on their clutch of eggs until they hatched. Modern farming methods meant that there was not usually any call for hens to produce their own chickens so broody hens were isolated in a small coop for a short period of time whereupon they rapidly returned to their egg producing ways.

But one hen, that day just about to enter the broody phase, was going to strike it lucky. "Alma" as David christened her, after the singer Alma Cogan whose unusual voice was enjoyed by both him and his mother when she performed on radio or television, was about to experience the joys of motherhood. Albeit, to an unusual family.

The next problem was getting the eggs and Granny thought of all her poultry-producing neighbours. The Andersons, her nearest neighbours kept turkeys while the Craigmiles, nearby, had a handful of ducks, but not to Granny's knowledge, a drake. The absence of such a father figure might work perfectly well in David and Peggy's household but would spell the end of "Project Duckling" before it began.

'It'll have tae be the Johnstones.' Granny stated categorically. 'You and Shada had better get yoursel's ower there efter you've had yir denner'.

David already knew old Mrs Johnstone who seemed to be the dominant figure in the small croft in question. She was, in fact, Sandy Stronach's mother in law, Sandy having married her elder daughter Doreen a number of years ago and fathered her three grandchildren at regular intervals thereafter.

The sound of a bicycle being abandoned against the side of the house brought the two plotters back to earth with a start. The porch door may or may not have been knocked upon, but seconds later the kitchen seemed full of the substantial figure that was Nurse Maggie Burnett.

Her complexion was scarlet from the exertion of her four-mile trek from Polknappie and the sweat was falling freely.

'Well, Elsie,' she gasped, 'Foo are yi the day?' and to David, 'Are you in ony better humour yet, loon? I've always said, Elsie,' she opined to Granny, 'It's the lack o' daylicht in them big toons, that maks a' body sae crubbit.'

From the kitchen window, David could see an ample supply of daylight. Nevertheless, he was beginning to feel exceedingly crabbit!

'You had better awa' and see your granda.' Granny said firmly, and to Maggie, 'Have you heard any more about your car?'

David correctly felt that he was being dismissed and slunk sulkily out of doors. So Nurse Burnett had indeed seen him today as she had implied yesterday. 'Big deal, had she no work to do?'

David decided not to join his grandfather, who had already been cutting peats for several hours, but planned to seek out Helen who had caught him so off guard at their chance meeting of last night.

'Or was it a chance meeting?' he asked himself, 'or did she know that the "Pirate Ship" would be his first port of call as usual?'

Their meeting had been short and they had not touched, although David was aware that if it had been an American movie, they would have embraced wholeheartedly. 'That would have been nice,' he decided.

He climbed a fence and dropped into a meadow belonging to the Home Farm. If he cut across diagonally he would rejoin the road some fifty yards from the cottage where Helen lived with her family.

With Shada following possessively at his heels, the attention of the grazing cattle was immediately aroused. As cattle have done for hundreds of years they careered towards them, intent at getting a better look at the dog. David was not quite the city slicker that people here sometimes seemed to imagine and knew he was quite safe. With exaggerated nonchalance he convinced himself it was no different from crossing Princess Street in heavy traffic and he stuck to his planned route, hopping on to the road just as the bravest cow, nose to the ground came within sniffing distance of the unconcerned Shada.

Erchie Sutherland, a morose individual with unfathomable mood swings was chief cattleman or head 'bailey' in charge of the Home Farm's dairy herd. He rose at three o'clock every morning to milk the cattle and retired again to bed sometime about mid morning. Helen was the oldest of his three children, one of whom invariably disturbed his daytime nap and perhaps contributed to his surly humour.

She must have been looking out of her window and was soon skipping along the road to see him. She looked happy. And very beautiful.

'Ar Jim lad!' she said, standing on one leg and leaning on an imaginary crutch. 'Pieces of eight! Pieces of eight!' she shrieked in perfect imitation of David's parrot noises of yesterday, before collapsing in a fit of giggles, on the grassy roadside verge.

David was confused. In the space of thirty seconds, Helen had excited and embarrassed him: just as she had done last night.

Now as she sat in the grass, her head and her hands on her knees, her faded blue dress half up her thigh, she seemed completely unaware of the effect she was having on David. Perhaps it was the year she had spent at the big school, perhaps it was because she now stretched over him by at least six inches, perhaps it was because she now seemed so remarkably like a young woman that he felt things had changed irrevocably. The easy, fun filled relationship they had enjoyed for six years seemed in jeopardy, things were moving on.

34

Perhaps it was that she wanted Elvis Presley and he just wanted his pal.

'Let's go to Mrs Hamilton's!' she said, dragging him to his feet and playfully thumping him on the shoulder. Just like before, she ran, Shada barked, and David ran too.

It was at Mrs. Hamilton's that they had first met, all those years ago.

Peggy had stopped for a blether with the Johnstone girls, and David, aged six, had wandered on. The marmalade kitten that crossed his path had been like the rabbit in "Alice's Adventures in Wonderland". David followed it and found himself in front of the strangest little house ever!

It was impossible to know if the house was occupied, although countless chickens pecked contentedly by the doorstep. The marmalade kitten had joined up with what was presumably its large extended family and some fifteen assorted cats stalked tiger-like and spat at each other in the sunlight. Every window in the house was covered, from the inside, with brown wrapping paper of the kind Peggy used on the parcels she occasionally sent home from Edinburgh. Could anyone live in a house like this?

David was lost and uncertain how long he had been missing from his mother. He prepared to do the obvious thing. He marched up to the weather-bleached door and prepared to knock.

'Dinna dae that!' a voice implored frantically from behind a honeysuckle bush. 'A mad witch bides in there!'

Mad witches and talking honeysuckle bushes! David was seriously afraid. As he started to run, he knew not where, a pair of tiny, grubby hands wrestled him to the ground and the comparative shelter of the bush.

'Would yi like an aipple?' she asked, offering a misshapen crab apple that looked positively disgusting.

Helen's clothes looked second or third hand and as in need of a wash as she was, but her grin spread from ear to ear and was entirely captivating. Thus began their friendship.

35

It was clear, that the youthful Helen had a very vivid imagination and was undaunted if her stories sometimes seemed implausible. David was impressed.

The owner of the house, for whom the name Mrs Hamilton seemed far too ordinary, was according to Helen indeed, both mad and a witch who never came out of doors, even to buy her groceries or tend her animals.

'And dae yi see that?' she pointed triumphantly to a considerable but unidentifiable stain which seemed to come from a skylight window and left a discoloured mark all the way to the guttering. 'That's faur she empties her Charlie!'

David knew that "Charlie" was the name many people used for their chamber pot or potty and if she really did empty it from her upstairs window, Helen must be right. Mrs Hamilton must clearly be mad, or a witch. Or both.

Without explaining precisely how she had managed it, Helen told how once she had actually seen inside the mysterious house, and it was like a palace!

'Gold and jewels everywhere' she explained, 'and nae a speck o' dust anywhere. They say she wis in shippin'.'

David knew that many big ships visited Leith, every day, but he had no idea that they contained such treasures. 'Perhaps,' he reasoned, 'some of the flats in the tenements where he lived, might be as palatial as this unusual croft house!'

'And then there's her loon.' Helen interrupted, referring to Mrs Hamilton's son. 'He hasnae been seen for years. My dad says he's clean aff his heid, but some folk says he's in the jile.' As if that was not dramatic enough, Helen leant forward into David's face and asked darkly, 'But then again, hiv yi ony idea fit witches pit in their pots o' soup?'

David had just decided that his new found pal must be the wisest seven year old in Scotland, when his mother suddenly appeared, breathing hard and in a state of some agitation.

'David, come here this minute,' she said in what sounded remarkably like a posh Edinburgh accent, and as she grabbed him more roughly than usual, David sensed that

36

mixture of anger and relief that parents reserve for those situations in which their offspring has taken unnecessary risks but survived intact.

'But Mum,' he said, unwisely desperate to share these strange happenings with her. 'There's a mad wifie in there, and – she's a witch!'

This revelation did not have the imagined effect. David was confused and disappointed as his mum grabbed him by the wrist and began to march him up the road.

'She is not mad!' Peggy retorted pointedly. David should have known better. As a trained psychiatric nurse, Peggy had strong views on mental illness and little time for many of the words other people used as a matter of course.

The journey back to Mossyhillock was likely to be a silent one, but David didn't care. Helen, who had mysteriously disappeared, at the first sign of Peggy's disapproval, had arranged to meet him on the following day to show him where a pair of wood pigeons had built their nest.

- 5 -

Going to the Dogs

David had quickly devoured his dinner, as his grandparents invariably called lunch, and with Shada, he headed for the Johnstones' croft and the duck eggs.

His earlier trip to Mrs Hamilton's with Helen had provoked many memories but led to no new adventures. Whatever she got up to, she was still getting up to it and Helen and David remained intrigued.

'Well, Shaddie,' said Mrs Johnstone, employing her usual habit of talking to the animal rather than the human. 'Fa's this you've got wi' yi the day?' And as if to demonstrate that the question was superfluous, 'I'm surprised that he's got time for the likes o' us. I thocht he would be too busy gaun to a' these gairden parties wi' the Queen. That's what happens in Edinburgh, yi ken.' She chortled at what she considered to be her wit, and as if to encourage her, Shada wagged her tail. 'Well, yi'd better bring him in'.

Having been brought into the tiny kitchen by Shada, David resisted the temptation to pass all his messages through her, and told Mrs Johnstone his requirements, face to face. She seemed impressed.

'Can you believe that, Shaddie?' she asked the dog. 'Quite the wee fermer we've got here. Yi niver see that deen nooadays. I mind before the quines were born we used to tak oot a' oor ain poultry, but we've niver tried it since.'

Shada gave the impression that she understood. David understood that a "quine" was a girl and that Doreen Stronach was Mrs Johnstone's elder daughter. It must have been nearly forty years since she had "taken oot" her own ducklings!

'Come on.' called the old lady. 'We'd better see if we've a bag for him.' Shada obediently followed her out, leaving David on his own.

On her return Mrs Johnstone was indeed carrying a bag in which David surmised was the all-important eggs. 'He'd

38

better be careful,' she told the dog. 'There's a fortnicht's worth o' breakfasts in there!'

As David thanked her profusely, she addressed him directly for the first time. 'It's nae as straightforward as yi micht think.' she told him. 'You dae exactly fit yir granny says if you wint tae mak a success o' this.'

David assured her that he would and with a whistle to Shada, had gone. When he reached the end of her path he turned and gave her a cheery wave.

'Fit dae yi' think. Joey?' she addressed the budgie that was dozing on its perch. 'Isn't he a richt good mannered loon?'

The track from Mrs Johnstone's croft was a typical farm road. It was narrow, in a bad state of repair and with overgrown hedges. It had been constructed, after a fashion, on the assumption that it would be used by pedestrians, the occasional horse and trap and the postie's bicycle.

On turning a bend therefore, David was astounded to see Sandy Stronach's familiar bus, gingerly edging its way along this most unsuitable of carriageways. According to his timetable, this was a free period for Sandy and he was indulging in his usual habit of using the bus as if it were his private car.

Sensing an opportunity to delay his inevitable meeting with 'the tiger' as he irreverently and privately called his mother in law, Sandy drew his bus to a halt.

'Afternoon Colonel' he smiled, raising his permanently gloved right hand in mock salute as soon as he had wound down his window. 'What brings you to this neck of the woods?'

David, clutching his precious bag of eggs, found himself almost crushed against a fierce looking dog rose bush, which bordered the only piece of grass verge not being occupied by the oversize bus. He returned Sandy's greeting but ignored his question. This chance meeting had provided him with an unexpectedly early opportunity to ask a few questions of his own.

As a way of introducing the subject, David nodded in the direction of the poster in the bus. 'Have you sold many tickets for your dance yet, Sandy?' he asked. Perhaps a little too eagerly, he followed up. 'Sandy, who are the Burma Star Association?'

Without turning a hair, Sandy completely changed the subject.

'I see Auld Random has still got that ugly auld dog o' his.' He said indicating towards Shada. The look on his face however, was one of affection.

Like most of the people in the district, Sandy routinely referred to David's grandfather as "Auld Random". Nicknames for farmers and other country dwellers were common and in the North East as in other farming communities, they often swapped their own name for that of their farm. Why, even the poet Robert Burns, was at one time known as "Rab Mossgiel" after the Ayrshire farm he worked with his brother.

Davy Gordon could therefore have expected to be called "Mossy" or even "Hillie" but his name came courtesy of Hitler and the BBC!

Throughout World War II, the large area of marshy and otherwise difficult to cultivate ground adjacent to Mossyhillock had been used as a "dummy airport". Sufficient partially concealed lights were assembled in such a way as to hopefully trick the German pilots into thinking they were over flying Aberdeen Airport at Dyce, a few miles to the west.

If successful, such a ruse would be as reassuring for the large population of Aberdeen as it would be unsettling for the few country dwellers such as Davy and Elsie who lived and worked in the immediate vicinity.

And one night, they got it right. Three bombs fell, very much in the middle of no-where although flying debris damaged one of the two farmhouses nearby. From a British point of view, the defensive strategy had been a success and the next day the BBC announced that three bombs had been dropped at random.

The site of the bomb holes and Davy Gordon were known as "random" from that day on!

'Hiv yi iver seen real dogs chasing a hare?' Sandy asked with the emphasis on *"real"*.

David shook his head, although he knew he was being less than truthful.

'Well then,' Sandy continued, 'you be at the crossroads to catch the seven o'clock bus, a week on Wednesday. Oh, and dinna tell onybody.'

David was intrigued, but unsure if he would have money for the fare, or where indeed he would be going and explained this to Sandy.

'It's nae wonder bus companies are gaun oot o' business ivry day.' he grinned. 'Jist be there!'

As Sandy reluctantly pulled off, David was left to make the short journey back to Mossyhillock, pondering the last time he had seen dogs chasing a hare. It was a secret that he had shared with no one.

Tony and Senga Togneri were cousins who both stayed a short distant from David and Peggy and were usually seen, when not at school, in the company of their grandfather, a short man in a fur-lined jacket. The cousins seemed to spend most of their time running messages between their grandfather and numerous strangers who would somehow know to accost them in the street.

Peggy had warned David never to get caught up in any of the Togneri's dubious activities, and, if he was honest, that was probably why he ended up accompanying them to the races.

The dog track was only a short distance from Leith Walk and attracted huge crowds to its regular greyhound racing evenings. Tony, who had been for some reason particularly friendly with David of late had asked him along and even arranged to have him slip in unobserved via a rear entrance. David was free to watch the races and if he wished, run a few errands for Old Man Togneri.

Papa Togneri was the first person they saw when they arrived at the track. He was standing on a box next to a poster

41

that read "Honest" Joe Green. 'Ooh, there's my Papa Sam!' yelled Tony excitedly.

David was enthralled at the greyhounds, each with a different coloured "jacket" on their backs and straining to get out of what looked like single celled cages. David could feel the excitement in the crowd rising as a mechanical "hare" sped along the side of the track on an electric rail. No sooner had it shot past the "cages" than their doors were flung open and the multi coloured greyhounds raced out in hot pursuit! The greyhound in the blue "jacket" which had impressed David whilst in its "cage" came last.

As the roars and groans of the crowd died down, David was aware of another commotion coming from the direction of Papa Togneri's box. A white-faced Tony and Senga were talking to a policewoman, while two policemen were questioning Joe or Sam. Someone who could only have been a plain clothed detective was hovering near by. Joe or Sam stood with his outstretched arms at his sides; he was showing the palms of his hands and shrugging his shoulders in a theatrical and unconvincing attempt to show that he was as honest as his poster proclaimed.

David started to cry.

It was then that a kindly face appeared from amongst the gawping onlookers. He wore a fur-lined jacket exactly like Papa Togneri but seemed somehow safe and reliable.

'I've never noticed you before, son.' he said. 'It's time you were out of here.' He pushed through to the back of the crowd, nodding once or twice to people who smiled at him, and pointed to a doorway similar to the one through which Tony and David had entered. 'Get out through there and don't stop running till you get home. And son,' he shouted to the fast disappearing David. 'Next time, - stick to the pictures!'

Almost a week later, when Tony next came to school, he took David aside. 'Papa says you must never tell your mother what happened the other night.' he said solemnly.

There was no chance of that!

As David finally arrived within sight of Mossyhillock, his precious eggs were yet again put in jeopardy. Not to mention his life!

A car, the first he had seen since leaving Aberdeen yesterday was approaching him at speed along the old farm road. The roar of an overworked engine suggested that it was still in first gear and its erratic motion reminded David of the jumping jack fireworks available at Guy Fawkes time. 'Kangaroo petrol!' he muttered to himself as he and Shada leapt for the safety of the corn yard.

To his amazement, as the car, which he recognised to be a brand new Morris Minor, raced by, he saw none other than Nurse Maggie Burnett fixed to the wheel, her face once again scarlet, her mouth hanging wide open, and her eyes staring in front but seeing nothing. She would never reach Polknappie!

Even more unlikely, for just one moment, he thought he heard his grandfather swear. Something he had never heard before.

Granda was not swearing when David ran the last few yards to the croft house but both he and Granny were in an almost unintelligible state of agitation. Next to the door, the remains of last year's peat stack was in disarray with peats scattered all over the place.

'And she's supposed to be educated.' groaned Granda before literally sinking to his knees.

Slowly, they related the story to David.

As had been planned for a number of weeks, Maggie had taken possession of the new car earlier that day, her large round proving unserviceable by bicycle. Unfortunately she had never driven a car since the day, seven years ago when she had somewhat surprisingly passed her driving test. Whatever the reason, she had decided to pay a social visit to Mossyhillock on her very first outing, and had somehow got there without undue mishap.

After a cup of tea, when she decided to leave, however, the car refused to start. Old Davy was no mechanic, and could only offer to push, although he was probably far too old for

43

such an activity. With Granny unable to help, Davy was grateful that the car was parked on a considerable incline even though it was facing the wrong way.

No problem, cars can be bump started in reverse and after given Maggie instructions, Davy put his shoulder to the front of the car and found it could be moved fairly easily, backwards, down the slope.

'Now!' Shouted Davy, as the car gathered speed. Maggie took her foot from the clutch. The car burst into life, and for the first time, Maggie realised she had a problem. She was reversing at speed, and quite frankly, couldn't really reverse slowly! Although Granda was not yet ready to admit it, the peat stack had been an ideal target, cushioning the impact in a way similar to the tyres built up round a Grand Prix track and minimising damage all round.

Luckily the car did not need to be pushed again, and it was Nurse Burnett's speedy retreat that David had witnessed earlier. 'And yes,' he convinced himself, 'he had heard Granda swearing!'

The retelling of the story helped demonstrate the funny side, and Granny's facial contortions suggested she was about to giggle. Just at the point that she could contain herself no longer, she caught Davy's eye and he too spluttered uncontrollably.

The old couple collapsed into each other's arms laughing out loud in a way that they hadn't done for years.

It had been a long day; David felt in his pocket for a sugar lump and slipped off to see Tibbie. |

- 6 -

Old Scotia's Grandeur

Not a drum was heard, not a funeral note,
As his corse to the rampart we hurried;
Not a soldier discharged his farewell shot,
O'er the grave where our hero we buried

David sat entranced, on the three-legged milking stool that had somehow made it into the house. He gazed up at his grandfather who, for once comfortable in his armchair, was enjoying the moment. Unlike the village of Balcrannie, the outlying dwellings did not yet receive electricity and the paraffin "Tilley" lamp remained unlit. What light there was, came from the dying sun and the smouldering peat fire.

An excellent night for secretly burying a fallen comrade, David reflected.

We buried him darkly at dead of night,
The sods with our bayonets turning,
By the struggling moonbeam's misty light
And the lanthorn dimly burning.

David's earnest request to his grandfather for information about the "Burma Star Association" had not elicited the response he had desired, but instead had prompted Davy to embark on one of their favourite pastimes, poetry.

'Granda,' said David, slipping effortlessly into the North East dialect that was literally his Mother's tongue, 'wis you iver a sodjer'?

His grandfather seemed to hesitate momentarily, and as he peered up at the suddenly aged face he loved so much, David thought he saw a tear. 'Nonsense,' he corrected himself, 'other people could shed enough tears to turn Princes Street Gardens back into the loch it had once been, but his granda, would never cry'!

45

'Na, laddie', the old man replied, his gnarled hand definitely wiping something away, 'I wis nivver that'. He paused, 'Maybe that's why we're baith here the nicht'!

David failed to pick up on that sentiment, 'Foo auld are yi, Granda?' he asked, although he was almost sure that he was sixty-four. Mental arithmetic was David's strong point, but he used his fingers to make sure. Granda would have been nineteen in nineteen fourteen, the year in what Miss Playfair called "The Great War" had started. How come he had missed out?

Davy Gordon's thoughts were on the same subject. "I micht hae been a sodjer," he sighed dolefully, "I so easily micht hae been".

David Henry Gordon was born in 1895 in the shadow of Bennachie in Aberdeenshire: his destiny to be a beast of burden.

David sensed his grandfather was back there now, and half intrigued, said nothing.

'Was it really fifty years ago?' the old man silently mused, 'that he had triumphantly strode the Garioch foothills. His short arms fully stretched at ninety degrees from his undernourished body, just reaching the man sized shafts of the ancient plough.' Frankly it was cruelty and he would cheerfully paralyse anyone that would visit such a fate on young David. But at fourteen, Davy was a ploughman, he had been left the school for nearly two years, and as he gazed southwards across the fertile fields where they told him lay the city of Aberdeen, his life seemed to be all mapped out for him.

Davy had liked the school and being somewhat brighter than many of his classmates he had managed to avoid many of the more savage leatherings that was the daily lot of the totally uneducated, probably uneducatable youths he had called his pals.

They'd suffered for him then and in a few short years, there would be France.

For a minute Davy wondered about the half demented "dominie" as head teachers were invariably called in North East Scotland, Auld "Shittie" White whose twin pleasures

46

seemed to be romantic poetry and state sanctioned child cruelty!

It was that same state that allowed children of large, poor families, to leave school a year early in order to contribute to the family budget, or at least get their meagre food rations somewhere else. When Davy left school he was only twelve but he left another four brothers and sisters to fly the Gordon flag in that two roomed centre of learning. Now there was only him and his half daft sister, Maisy, still alive. He must visit her in that place in Aberdeen sometime soon he decided.

'Granda, fit aboot The Charge O' the Light Brigade?' David had indulged his grandfather's reverie long enough and now wanted to hear the poem they both loved.

Half a league, half a league,
Half a league onward,
All in the valley of Death
Rode the six hundred.
'Forward, the Light Brigade!
Charge for the guns!' he said:
Into the valley of Death
Rode the six hundred.

'Forward, the Light Brigade!'
Was there a man dismay'd?
Not tho' the soldiers knew
Someone had blunder'd:
Their's not to make reply,
Their's not to reason why,
Their's but to do and die:
Into the valley of Death
Rode the six hundred.

'I *could* have been a sodjer!' The old man almost spoke the words aloud, but instead continued to declaim his favourite tale of working class heroism and military blunder. Was it always thus?

Davy reckoned he must have had about eight winters of sixteen-hour days, calf high fields of mud and endless, backbreaking, chilblain inducing weeks of turnip harvesting. Pu'ing neeps was the Doric words for it and Davy was sure if the Russian "heidbummers" ever wanted a change of job for the hundreds of thousands of their countrymen that they had working the Siberian salt mines, a neep park near Oldmeldrum might be the ideal solution!

Had Davy ever heard of the Arch Duke Franz Ferdinand, his murder would scarcely have interfered with the daily summertime grind, and as autumn brought the inevitable war, the North East was immersed in its labour intensive hairst.

But that winter was different for all at Gushet Neuk. The weather was just as inhospitable, the days just as long and the turnip harvest as soul destroying as ever. But in the short hours between bedding down the horse at ten and hauling himself out of bed at five thirty, something was happening!

Neighbouring farm lads met together as they had always done for a smoke or a blether, while those with romance in mind would struggle along the muddy cart tracks to wherever the objects of their ardour might be employed as a "kitchie deem" or domestic servant. And whenever people met, the subject, inevitably turned to, - *war*.

Unlike many of his companions, Davy had a fair idea of where France was, but until now, his chances of ever going there, he rated as no better than going to the moon. As for the Germans whom he was now supposed to hate: weren't the Royal Family mostly German and weren't we supposed to respect them?

It was one Saturday night in February, as a few of them struggled to play pontoon by the light of their woodbines that Davy dropped his bombshell. He was going to enlist!

He had anticipated the likely need for more troops even before the government recruiting campaign featuring Lord Kitchener was fully in swing, and it stood to reason, he mused,

48

that a field in France was bound to be less muddy and inhospitable than one in Aberdeenshire, and what if he had to swap his hoe for a rifle? No one in the parish could throw a stone as hard or as far as he could, perhaps he was a natural!

Next winter, he would celebrate his victory and demob in Paris, and then, - whatever!

Wullie Reid, the orra loon, or young general labourer from "Southies", grasped at the idea even although he was only seventeen. For the first time ever, he contemplated a life that did not involve the daily toil of farm work. By morning, Tam Simpson and Robbie Greenhowe, both horsemen at Gushets were on board, although Robbie was unsure how his girlfriend, Elsie might react. Clearly it was a delicate subject.

Late that Sunday night, as Davy completed, the seventeen miles round hike to his parents' cottage and back, the party was complete. His younger brother, Peem, the favourite of all the family, had decided to join in the adventure.

'Aye, he micht be a dab hand at the poetry,' the reverie was broken by Granny, who had appeared in the room with a half loaf and three cups, 'but ask him aboot his Latin!' She stooped over the fire, and satisfying herself that the kettle was boiling, made the tea. Not that it mattered, thought David, his granny's tea was legendary: strong, with large leaves invariably floating on the top, of indiscriminate temperature and invariably repulsive. If anyone else in the world presented him with such a concoction, David would have spat it out, but Granny's tea was part of what made him feel so comfortable and safe in that dilapidated old croft house.

She was making heavy weather of preparing the tea, but David thought he spotted a glint of triumph in her eye as with a hint of the theatre, she lightly thumped the teapot on the table.

'Mensa, mensa, mensam,' she declaimed, and helpfully translated, not for the first time. 'table, oh table, table,' she grinned, for her school was equally small and she too had left at twelve, but not before she had been given a smattering of Latin, of which she was immensely proud.

49

David thought about August for the first time in days. He was going to take Latin when he went to Broughton Street High School and he was unsure of how he felt about it. Whatever the benefits of learning it might be, all David knew was that it was a dead language, and try as he might, he could never imagine himself being so intimate with a bit of furniture that he would need to address it as 'Oh table.'

David had lived through many such good-humoured exchanges in the past, and as he lavished the new made butter on his bread, he could see Granda was smiling. Clearly he did not begrudge his wife her linguistic one-upmanship.

Granny's face seemed unusually grey and for the first time, David noticed how much older she seemed this year. Granda looked concerned. But neither spoke to David. David said nothing, because that, he felt was what was expected of him.

'I think I'll awa ben the hoose,' she grimaced, ' and let you twa get on wi' yir poetry.' She disappeared into the bedroom, which she had shared with Davy for nearly forty years.

'She's a martyr to hertburn.' smiled Granda, a trifle too quickly.

They did not feel like poetry, yet neither of them broached their concern for Granny. David felt obliged to break the silence. 'We could try Stevenson, I suppose?' he ventured.

Granda, started, pleased it seemed, for a chance to change the focus of his attentions and spoke the words he had used so often in the past.

Under the wide and starry sky,
Dig the grave and let me lie,
Glad did I live and gladly die,
And I laid me down with a will.

This be the verse you grave for me:
Here he lies where he longed to be;
Home is the sailor, home from the sea,
And the hunter home from the hill.

David shivered. For once, he wished his Granda had chosen a more cheerful poem.

-7 -

Let the Sun Shine

The day had dawned early at Mossyhillock, and David was impatient to get started. He had been breakfasted before eight; some three hours earlier than might have been the case had he been at home, and now awaited his granny. Shada too, seemed aware that this was no ordinary day.

The old woman, her heartburn of the previous night long since forgotten, seemed relaxed and eager to commence.

'Come on, Fermer,' she grinned. 'There's work to be done.'

They had already decided that the old hen house nearest to the cornyard would be the ideal antenatal ward for the broody hen and her expected offspring. Within it, and on an old table some three feet from the ground was and old wooden box. The faded lettering, announced 'Canadian Mac Red' in acknowledgement to its original use as a container for imported apples, and it seemed just about the right size for a hen and a clutch of eggs.

'Perhaps some straw,' David thought, 'would make excellent bedding for the adoptive mum.'

Granny smiled indulgently. 'There's a lot more to it than that.' she said. 'Fetch me a spade!'

On the grassy patch just outside the hen house, Granny carefully measured a square, its size, exactly that of the bottom of the old apple box. With David's and Shada's incredulous eyes firmly glued to her every move, she skilfully dug up the divot which contained about two or three inches of soil, and inserted it in the box.

'The eggs need a certain amount of moistness,' she explained in answer to David's unasked question, 'and this is how they've done it since Adam was a bairn. Noo you can get your straw.'

But even that was not the end of it. Before placing the twelve eggs in the nest, Granny produced a crayon like marker from her pocket and placed a miniscule spot on each of them.

'If the eggs are going to hatch,' she explained, 'they have to be turned daily, so that the whole egg gets a uniform heat. The hen will know that, but sometimes nature needs a wee hand. That's where you come in, David.'

David was rapidly learning that there was more to "taking oot" ducklings than just sitting back and waiting. For the next twenty-eight days (ducks never seemed to vary, he was assured), he would have a crucial part to play in the birthing process.

'Alma,' Granny confidently predicted, 'would take to her new role like a duck to water.' David was unsure if the joke was intended, so said nothing. He had learned sufficient this morning already, to not be surprised when Granny explained that various complications might set in.

Alma's own health and well-being could apparently prove an issue. Like mothers everywhere, it seemed, she was likely to put her youngsters' needs very much before her own. Thinking of Peggy, David had the good grace to blush on hearing this piece of wisdom.

In Alma's case this could well mean that she would stay on the nest indefinitely, ignoring her own need for food, water and exercise to such an extent that she may become ill.

Once a day, then, David would have to visit the hen house, and after ensuring that there was a supply of food and water readily available he would have to lift Alma from her nest in the hope that this would prompt her to partake. With her now safely out of the way, David would quickly check the mark on each egg to see if it had been rotated during the course of the previous twenty-four hours. This would be the "wee hand" that nature might require from David, as it would be his task to rotate any egg about which Alma may have accidentally forgotten. He would then retreat from the scene for some fifteen minutes to allow Alma to eat and drink her fill.

The nest was deliberately raised off the ground to help safeguard it from predators such as rats and this would also make it less likely that Alma would return to it immediately to the detriment of her own health. It was likely, therefore, that David's task on returning to the hen house would be to return her to the nest and settle her down for the day ahead.

David realised that this project, dreamt up over winter in Edinburgh, would place a considerable responsibility on his shoulders during the next few weeks, but he was looking forward to the challenge.

Mission set in motion; grandmother and grandson emerged from the hen house to the reassuring spectacle that life was going on as usual. Maggie Burnett's car was parked (passably) close to the front porch, Davy Gordon was cheerfully chewing the Swiss milk tablet she had given him as way of an apology and Tibbie was boisterously parading the corn yard in anticipation of a rare day's work.

Hay making was a vital part of the summer routine at Mossyhillock and as the well-known proverb so rightly attested, it has to be done while the sun shines. Providing sufficient foodstuffs to overwinter their livestock was a perennial challenge to farmers everywhere, and hay along with turnips and the more modern silage was a vital ingredient in this endeavour.

This year's crop had been mown before the start of David's holiday and had enjoyed reasonable sunshine over the past few days to allow the drying process to begin. The task today was to gather it together into mini ricks or "coals" of about six feet in height. These in turn would be carted home a few weeks later and combined to form the more permanent ricks in which they would be finally stored.

Vital to today's task would be the mechanical, two-wheeled rake, which would greatly speed up the gathering process. Here for once, Fergie had no part to play. As farmers gradually modernised, the old horse drawn implements became redundant and had to be replaced, or when money was scarce, ingeniously adapted, for use by the usurping tractor.

Of all Davy's implements, the rake and the smaller of his box carts were the two that had not been altered, and so today, Tibbie reigned supreme.

As Granda attached the leather harness to the giant Clydesdale and slipped the shafts of the old rake into position, he was performing a task that had been done in an identical manner for generations. But the times were definitely a changing. When the century had begun, literally thousands of horses strode majestically throughout the vast number of fields in the northeast farming communities. Now, in the parish of Balcrannie at least, only Tibbie and old Davy remained. If either one of them gave up now, a way of life would have passed forever.

Tibbie ambled towards the waiting hay, scarcely aware of the rake that she was trailing behind her, and if she knew that it was young David who sat proudly aloft on its only seat, she gave no sign of complaint. Granda walked by her head; ready to influence or encourage her in any way he could, while David loosely held the reins in both hands.

His job was to shout instructions and apply pressure to the reins when he wanted Tibbie to stop or start, and to use a lever to operate the rake to firstly gather sufficient hay and then deposit it on a heap in the ground.

Shada raced ahead excitedly, covering three times as much ground as everyone else and examining every tuft of grass for a fleeing field mouse or, the big one, a startled rabbit.

David's thoughts flitted briefly towards Leith Walk and his many good pals there. What would they with their matinee film performances and television sets make of it all? Would they be envious, or would they ridicule him and his rural ways? The question seemed irrelevant. None of them could imagine the secret life of David Robert Gordon.

His reverie was disturbed with a start, as Tibbie and the rake stopped suddenly, just at the spot where David had been about to deliver his well rehearsed 'Whoa!'

Obviously, it was unnecessary. Granda chuckled indulgently and ruffled the old horse's mane. He could have sworn that Tibbie winked back at him. These youngsters had a lot to learn!

The sun was pleasantly warm and the work not overly hard. Man and boy toiled for the most part silently, their two favourite animals usually within touching distance and it felt, almost equal partners in the enterprise. Nature was all around.

However pleasant the task, the promise of a break and some nourishment will invariably make it better. The "fly" cup was an important part of the working day at Mossyhillock and one of which David wholeheartedly approved. As a toddler, he had "helped" his mother or grandmother carry the tea and scones or jam sandwiches to whichever part of the field his grandfather was working. The tea would be carried, usually in a bottle and drunk from an enamel mug while the bread and scones, usually called the "piece" oozed blackcurrant or rhubarb jam.

David's instincts told him that it must soon be "fly time", and almost on cue, a figure appeared from the croft house laden down as usual with the hungry men's rewards.
But today was different. Both workers could see, almost immediately, that it was not Granny that was approaching them and soon to his delight, David recognised Helen. As a rule Helen did not come to the croft or have many dealings with Granny and Granda and her presence here, however pleasurable, needed an explanation. And one was immediately forthcoming.

'Hi folks' she said in a distinctly unBalcrannie accent which grated on Granda's nerves. 'I just dropped in to see if you were doing anything special, David, and Mrs Gordon said she was feeling a bit tired after a' the excitement with the hen. She asked if I would deliver your fly for you. I hope that's ok Mr Gordon?'

'That's very nice of you, Lass.' said old Davy, slightly regretting his earlier uncharitable thoughts.

'That's just brilliant of you,' giggled David, 'Lass!'

Davy and David eagerly attacked the foodstuff and thirstily drank their tea. It was quite a logistical exercise. Tea, no sugar and plenty milk for Davy, tea, two sugars and milk for David, bread and rhubarb jam for Davy, bread and blackcurrant jam for David. Bread, butter and no jam for Shada, dry bread and a sugar lump for Tibbie.

Helen had nothing and that seemed entirely natural. In all the forty odd years that Granny had taken Davy's "piece" out to the fields for him, she had never taken anything for herself. Presumably she ate earlier or later. Or not at all.

The short break was much appreciated. Old Davy lay on his back, momentarily marvelling at the beautiful summer sky. The youngsters whispered and giggled a short distance away.

'Fit do you think o' Cliff Richard?' he heard Helen ask David and strained to hear his reply.

None was forthcoming. David, like his grandfather, had never heard of Cliff Richard.

It was time to start work again. Despite his hard work in the first part of the morning it seemed clear that David's mind was now on other things. 'Nae hairm in that.' reasoned Granda, well satisfied with David's earlier contribution.

'I think I can manage the rest o' this misel',' he offered. 'If you two young eens want to rin awa and play.'

The word "play" momentarily annoyed David, but the offer was too good to refuse. He playfully threw a handful of hay at Helen who had just gathered the tea things together. Balancing the tray in front of her she took off towards the house giggling happily, her long legs propelling her effortlessly across the grass. David (and Shada) was in hot pursuit.

Old Davy seemed strangely at ease as he mounted the rake and sat down on what had been David's seat. With merely the hint of a 'Gee up!' and the slightest flick of the rein, Tibbie started to trundle forward.

Davy was alone with his thoughts of yester evening. Where was he again?

'Ah, yes. February 1915.'

- 8 -

The King's Shilling

It was scarcely daylight when the five of them set out that morning. The cattle had all been looked after and were warm and dry in their byres or sheltering at the side of the fir trees in the high park. The farmer, W. J. Ogston J.P. was jumping up and down with rage as they took their leave, threatening to have them out of their bothy that very night. But their minds were firmly made up. It was 1915 and they were going to enlist.

Robbie, Tam and Wullie had one old bike between them, taking turns to crank the pedals while one sat on the crossbar and the other perched precariously on the carrier above the rear wheel.

Davy and his younger brother Peem were marginally luckier. They shared the bicycle they had borrowed from Eddie Baxter who had just become engaged to their oldest sister, Gladys. Eddie came from mining stock in Fife and his parents were trying hard for him to take a job in mining until after the war was over; it was what he knew best. But Gladys thought Fife was 'afa far awa' and didn't want to go.

Mercifully, they could leave their bicycles at the station at Inverurie some five miles away, from where they would take the train to Aberdeen, fifteen more miles along the river Don. Only Robbie had ever been to Aberdeen before, to see the football team play at Pittodrie. He had not been impressed.

'A dirty, orra hole o' a place.' he had described it, 'Wi' horse dung a' ower the streets, and ill fed looking bairns at ivry corner.'

They had not been prepared for what they found at Inverurie. Their plans were not unique. Men of all shapes and sizes were noisily waiting to board the already crowded train and the atmosphere was like the aftermath of a "feein' market"or hiring fair when spirits were high and whisky had been drunk.

'All aboard for Wipers!' yelled one fresh faced potential recruit of about fifteen years of age. His two older brothers had already enlisted though their eagerly awaited second letter home appeared to be overdue.

'You're country needs yooou!!!' screamed a five foot nothing fifty-year-old pointing Kitchener style at a pregnant cat skulking behind some empty barrels. Encouraged by the good-humoured roars from the fifty or so likeminded individuals on the platform he continued. 'There's nae a bloody German in a' .... ,' he paused to think of a suitably dramatic location, ... 'Germany!' he finally roared, 'that could last ten minutes in a straight fecht wi' ony o' us here!'

Encouraged by the crowd, he dropped to one knee and using his imaginary rifle started shooting imaginary Germans from the rooftops.

As the beer he had been drinking began to take its inevitable effect on his bladder, he was cheered uproariously all the way to the corrugated iron makeshift toilet near the station's entrance.

When he returned, the train had gone and the platform was completely empty.

Nevertheless, Davy had been impressed with all he'd seen. 'Where else but the Garioch', he pondered, 'could produce such a fine body of men with such little effort?' He felt relaxed and extremely confident.

He paid scant attention to the city of Aberdeen on this his first visit. All of them were carried away on the euphoria that propelled them to the recruiting booths in the Castlegate where the scenes at Inverurie were multiplied many times over.

No barriers were put in the way of those wishing to volunteer. Medical examinations were perfunctory and background checks non-existent. Neither Wullie nor Peem, both officially underage, had any difficulty in being accepted even although Peem had chosen an imaginary birthday only two months after Davy's real one. They were next to each other in the queue and were clearly brothers but no one seemed to notice. Or care.

Basic training would begin on Thursday!

The remainder of their time in Aberdeen was spent celebrating their freedom from the tyranny of bad tempered farmers and drinking to their decision to become a Gordon Highlander! Jokes were told, stories swapped and outrageous plans made for life after the inevitable victory. If anyone had any misgivings, they were kept completely under wraps.

****

Much later, back in a quieter Inverurie, they retrieved the two borrowed bicycles, bought fish suppers and headed for the country and home.

But not if P.C. Johnny Summers had anything to do with it! 'Three on a bike!' he bellowed as he chanced across them on the outskirts of the town. 'And no lights! You're coming wi'me lads. I've niver seen onything like it!'

On an other night, maybe, tonight, - no chance! With a good few yards of a start and youth on their side they sped into the darkness. Someone yelled 'Race you! Flat feet!' and all hooted with laughter. It had been that kind of day!

Round the first corner however, emergency plans had to be made. Only Tam and Wullie had ever actually ridden a bike before today, and anyway, they were by far the most athletic. Robbie, Peem and Davy had to go, and go they did. As P.C. Summers rode furiously past, the three pals rolled down the grass verge on the side of the road into a deep-sided ditch with two inches of water at the bottom. They found they could stand up easily and if they were careful, they could just about keep their feet dry. They lit their woodbines and laughed and laughed.

How far would P.C. Summers go in pursuit of his master criminals? How long would a maximum ten-mile cycle run take? What was the going rate of fine for riding three on a bike, having no lights and fleeing from arrest? Who had accused the policeman of having flat feet?

They didn't know. But it must have been at least two hours before they dared climb out of the ditch to make the long journey back to the farm on foot.

*****

The Sunday dawned, cold and most disagreeably damp. Davy felt delicate from the beer and somewhat stiff from the episode in the ditch. He dreaded W.J. Ogston's reaction to his news that he had enlisted, but first things first. The beasts needed mucked out and fed. Who would do that next Sunday?

Davy had been doing the work for years, and despite his frailties the cattle in the byre were soon clean, fed and watered. All that remained was to take the turnips up to those hardier beasts that were wintering out of doors in the high field by the fir trees. The daily supply of turnips was essential, as grass at that time of year was practically non-existent.

Davy yoked the box cart, already full of turnips to the somewhat disinterested Mavis, a twenty something year old mare of undistinguished breeding.

More than anything, it would be the animals that Davy would miss when in France. He had names for them all. From Horatio, the one eyed cat to Harvey, the Shetland born pedigree bull in the high park. From Annabelle, his favourite milk cow, to Sophie, the over fed rat that would sometimes waken him by scurrying across his body as he lay in the bothy that was his home. Davy had first heard the name "Sophie" a few months ago and taken an instant liking to it.

Mavis knew the routine. Once in the high park she waited until Davy detached the "back door" of the box cart and scrambled aboard. On a single command, she started to edge slowly forward entirely on her own initiative, while Davy, armed with a graip or four pronged fork began scattering the turnips to the waiting cattle.

The attack was as unexpected and devastating as if the Kaiser's finest henchman had delivered it. And equally injurious to health!

Harvey, usually content to wait his turn, had lowered his head and charged. The force with which he hit the box cart was so severe that it overturned it and poor Mavis completely. Davy took the full force of the overturning cart on his left leg and the crack of breaking bone was heard by Wullie Reid, similarly employed, three fields away, in the neighbouring "Southies".

Davy was trapped, almost completely under the cart, but a sufficient portion of his upper back protruded to seemingly enrage Harvey even further and to provide him with a sitting target. Davy, fighting for breath and rapidly losing consciousness was to later recall that Harvey had charged three more times before, as inexplicably as he had first attacked, he bellowed ferociously and retreated to the shelter of the nearby fir trees.

Davy recalled little else of that Sunday, and was even unsure if the little he could remember had actually happened or merely been imagined by him. He remembered a stretcher and lots of people, he remembered a blustering W. J. Ogston J.P. screaming that he was ruined and incredibly he thought he remembered an immaculately dressed P. C. Summers orchestrating his first aid.

He remembered the agonising screams of his faithful pal, Mavis, a stranger in a suit, a single gunshot and silence.

*****

It was almost dark. Davy had been dozing fitfully against the most uncomfortable of odds. A rubber tube was stuck in his chest with the other end attached to a huge jar on the floor. His left leg was in a crude splint and his head covered in a bandage. The ward was full of individuals with a variety of equally horrible injuries.

'Here yi' are.' said Peem, proffering a large bottle of stout. 'I thocht I wasnae gaun ti' find you.' "It's Wednesday nicht.' he said ominously. Tomorrow was Thursday and the friends, reduced in number but not in patriotic fervour, would start their basic training. Robbie and Tam lurked at the end of the ward. Wullie had stayed outside in the street. He was afraid of blood.

'I'm so, so sorry that your nae gaun to be wi' us,' said Peem, 'It being your idea in the first place. They say we'll be helping oot the French sodgers,' he continued. 'It will be a' ower before you get back on yir feet.

'The Auld Alliance,' thought Davy, struggling to concentrate, but vaguely remembering one of "Dominie" White's history lessons. He was still unable to make any coherent reply to his brother.

'I've been thinking,' continued Peem, a little too quickly. 'This war is the chunce folk like us hiv been waiting for. I'm nae coming back here efter it's finished. Whit do yi' say aboot New Zealand, Davy? Sunshine and sheep, Davy, and a chunce for folk like us ti mak' something o' oorsel's.'

Davy nodded from behind his bandages. New Zealand sounded just fine. For the first time in his life, Peem bent forward and kissed his older brother on the cheek. 'Duty calls,' he mumbled.

'Oh Davy,' he turned and asked, 'Wis it you that accused Johnny Summers o' ha'ing flat feet? Fae fit Robbie Greenhowe tells me I think yi micht be due him an apology.'

Davy had drifted back to sleep, so didn't see his brother's final farewell or hear of what Robbie had seen on that fateful Sunday.

After the accident, Robbie had realised that there were plenty of people to accompany Davy to wherever he was going, and with a feeling of intense compassion towards the now lifeless Mavis, he went back to the farm to find something to cover her body until next morning. He returned with two huge corn sacks, which he felt would fit the bill. Suddenly, his attention was drawn to the clump of fir trees and the unlikely chain of events taking part behind them.

The whimpering W.J. Ogston J.P. was suspended by the collar of his jacket to a small branch, his feet dangling some eighteen inches from the ground. The furious, P.C. Summers, his face scarlet had both hands on the farmer's throat.

'Davy's fault?' he roared. 'I told you two months ago to get rid of that bull after it went for the roadman. You should be charged with attempted murder you old fool!'

'I am a Justice of the Peace,' whined Ogston. 'You can't speak to me like that, I have a good mind to send for your boss, before you ruin me completely!'

'You listen to me you auld bag of wind. Justice of the Peace or no, I'll get a train load of bosses to come oot fae the toon and kick the shit oot o' that fat belly o' yours if that killer bull is no in the knacker's yard tomorrow!

And oh, there'll be doctors and the hospital to pay for. I'm warning you Ogston,' he snarled. 'This episode had better not cost Davy Gordon a penny. It could have cost him his life.' He lifted the spluttering farmer back to earth.

'Your Honour,' he finished sarcastically, as adjusting his hat, he stormed away.

'I take it you'll have got those lichts on your bike sorted, Greenhowe,' he barked, as he strode past the tree behind which, Robbie had thought he was hiding.

Harvey was never seen again and Davy received no bill for his lengthy care and treatment.

Making Waves

David sat on the banks of the small burn or brook, and gazed admiringly at Helen. She was stretched out at the water's edge, lying flat on her tummy, her right hand submerged. The silence was total.

'You've got to tickle them, David,' she had explained many times before as she tried to teach him the art of "guddlin" trout.

David was a keen but as yet totally unsuccessful pupil.

'Here she goes, again.' She giggled girlishly as she rapidly removed her hand from the water still clutching a fair sized specimen of brown trout, which she deposited on the bank beside the other two which she had already caught. This was no mean feat since the slippery nature of the fish and its propensity to wriggle and squirm meant that it could be dropped at any time. If left too near the edge, it could, snake-like, find its way back to the life saving water. Many a prize specimen had been lost due to a moment's carelessness at this late stage.

Helen looked radiant. 'Your dinner, I believe, sir,' she beamed, as standing up she readjusted her dress so that it once again almost reached her knees.

David admiration knew no bounds. He doubted if there was a girl in the whole of Edinburgh who could guddle trout. He doubted if there was a girl in the whole of Edinburgh who could match Helen in any other way either.

Ever since their first meeting six years ago the two had been close pals and although their habit of getting into trouble meant their friendship didn't always meet with the grown ups' approval neither seemed to care.

In the early years, despite the somewhat exaggerated fears of his grandparents, David and Helen often met by this burn.

'Dinna you be coming hame drooned, noo, Laddie,' Granny would often warn, 'Fit on earth wid I tell yir mither if that happened?' And when David laughed at her concerns, 'You can droon in two inches o' watter, yi' ken.'

But they never did. They did, however, meet Malky Munroe and that was bad enough.

They must have been ten and eleven when that particular adventure enfolded two summers ago.

Malky was old, at least fifteen, tall and somewhat gangly. He had been fishing seriously with his home made rod for about fifteen minutes before he spoke to the two gawping children. 'Why don't you two buzz off? He grunted. 'This is my bit o' watter. I found it first.'

David prepared to leave. The young man seemed to have a point and it was a cardinal rule of his that you never started an argument that you couldn't win. But Helen had far too much spirit in her to ignore such a challenge from a mere stranger.

'Really,' she said, in an accent that she believed sounded incredibly upper crust. 'You *found* water in a burn? How extraordinary!' The youth, unsure of what was happening, visibly reddened. 'As far as I ken,' Helen continued in her native dialect, 'this is nae the Dee nor the Spey. Naebody owns watter, roon about here, but if they did, it widnae' be you. This loon's granda wid own it, he owns the grun roon aboot here'.

It was David's turn to change colour. 'Only fourteen acres of it.' He wanted to whisper to Helen but felt that she may not have welcomed his intervention. Malky however seemed impressed.

'I dinna ken why, I'm wasting my time, in a puddle like this,' he stated. 'Me being a real fisherman!'

Helen was in her element. 'A real fisherman?' she queried with mock reverence. 'That will be for yir piece, I take it.' She nodded towards the empty basket at the side of the burn. Helen could see that Malky's sandwiches were in a brown paper bag in his jacket and Malky knew that she could see them. The basket was clearly to carry his non-existent catch!

Malky was no longer enjoying his afternoon's leisure. 'I dinna ken why I came here in the first place,' he grumbled, gathering his bits and pieces. 'Jesus Christ himsel' couldna get fish oot o' a chunty pot like this! Cheerio.'

Helen allowed him to walk six or seven paces away. 'Excuse me Captain Birdseye,' she called, using her upper crust voice again. 'I don't think we got your name.'

The youth walked a little further before turning round. 'Its Malky.' He said. 'Malky Munroe, and really I've nae time to speak tae children.'

Helen ignored his emphasis on children. 'Going to get something for the tea, are you?' She smiled triumphantly. 'It's a peety there's nae a chip shop in Balcrannie, for that's the only place you'll get ony fish the day!'

Malky had clearly had enough of this obnoxious little girl and the silent boy who grinned at everything she said, all of which was calculated to demean him even further.

'I was just thinking,' she continued, 'with you being a real fisherman and that. It might be a wee bit embarrassing to go home wi' that basket of yours empty. Whit say you tae me giving you a wee hand?'

Malky was silently fuming but said nothing. Helen took that for a "yes". 'First things first,' she smiled. 'We've got to find, a decent spot.' She shook her head sadly at the spot where Malky had been standing, much to the discomfort of the permanently red faced youth. 'A real fisherman,' she said, shaking her head yet again. 'Ah this is better,' she nodded, once they had gone a few yards upstream. She dropped to the ground, and lying flat on her tummy, slipped her right hand into the water.

Fifteen minutes later she handed him the second brown trout that she had successfully "guddled". 'Stick them in your basket,' she grinned. Then as she eyed his jar of bait, 'You maybe better droon a couple o' these worms, in case onybody 's coonting them.'

67

Malky shuffled from one foot to the other. He wasn't sure why he felt the need to offer two kids an explanation, but he did so anyway. 'Look I'm sorry aboot earlier on,' he said, 'but I come from Balcrannie just as much as you do. My father has the salmon fishing, down at the beach. So you see, I honestly am a real fisherman.' He had the grace to blush a little as he continued. 'But maybe nae a very good ane,' he conceded, nodding towards the basket.

This made immediate sense to David. Although he had never met a Balcrannie fisherman, he knew they existed. The coast around the Scottish shore was divided up into sections and salmon fisherman had the right to net salmon off their own particular patch throughout the appropriate season. David had seen their nets set in the water when he had visited the beach with his mother. Balcrannie beach was renowned as being one of the best in Scotland. His mother explained how the fisherman rowed out to claim their catch when the tide was right, and how they were vulnerable to poachers once the nets were within wading distance from the shore.

It was a fact, David had already observed at his tender age, that the farming and the fishing communities seldom seemed to mix, and thus Malky was both a neighbour and a stranger, simply because of how his father earned his living.

Malky spoke again, addressing his question mainly at Helen. 'Dae yi' ken fit a wake is?' he asked.

Helen looked blank but David thought he knew. He could just recall the death of the Togneri cousins' grandmother some two years ago when he was about eight. Afterwards, Tony had regaled him at great lengths about the party that had followed her burial at Mount Vernon Cemetery. The most wonderful food had been on offer, and if Tony was to be believed, uncles and even aunts had hit the whisky with a vengeance and all had taken part in a communal rendering of "Jailhouse Rock" at the bus stop after they had been thrown out of the pub at closing time.

Most distasteful, David had thought and wasted no time in telling his mother just that.

'It's just their wye, son,' she had said tolerantly, but David knew that she secretly agreed with him.

Malky had listened carefully to David's experience of wakes and Helen seemed suitably impressed. Her parents neither drank nor sang, at bus stops or anywhere else.

'I suppose it's a bit like that,' Malky conceded. 'Bit my grannies have baith been deid for years. Its nae a granny we're seein' off tonight: it's a boat!'

He explained how for fishermen, their boat practically had a life and a personality of her own; perhaps that was why they always called it "she" rather than "it." Even although their work took place close to the shore, it was the boat that delivered their livelihood, and if an unexpected storm blew up, the skipper could only ever be as good as the craft he was steering. The boats had to be meticulously maintained especially during the close season and with a bit of luck a fisherman could hope to get twenty to thirty years out of her. The boat that was being "seen off" tonight was the "Mary-Belle IV" and she had given sterling service to Malky's family for some twenty-seven years.

'My uncle, Big Malk, is coming to pick me up in his shooting brake in about half an hour,' explained Malky. 'Would yi' like to come to the wake?'

Malky had been looking mainly at Helen and her response was immediate. 'Baith o' us?' she asked, nodding at David. 'We micht well consider it.'

'Oh well,' said Malky. 'If I have the organ grinder, I might as well tak' the monkey as well.'

David had never heard that expression before, and sensed that it might not be complimentary to him, but he didn't care. He was going to a wake!

Big Malk and his shooting brake, a Morris Minor that seemed half car, half van, duly arrived, bang on time. He looked every inch a fisherman in his long wellington boots turned over at the tops and his large chunky jersey. His ample tummy spilled over the top of his trousers and his tousled red hair was unfashionably long. Confusingly, he was several inches shorter than his nephew, Malky, otherwise known,

69

David presumed as "Little Malk". It would not always have been so.

The children clambered aboard without a moment's thought or hesitation.

The beach, now that the sun had gone down, was different from how David remembered it. The venue for the wake was somewhat removed from the beaten track used by holidaymakers. But there in a little clearing amongst the sand dunes, stood one of the biggest bonfires he had ever seen! Or it would be a bonfire once it was lit. Its base was built from old fish boxes and a couple of tree trunks that had obviously been rescued from the sea. It was piled high with anything that would burn and right on top, almost twice as high as the tallest man present, was the upturned Mary-Belle IV, which despite her grand sounding name, seemed to be little more than a slightly oversized rowing boat.

Makeshift tables had been erected on elderly looking fish barrels, and plates were piled high with roast potatoes and a variety of Balcrannie's best home-grown vegetables. Two roast chickens, some sausages and dozens of kippers completed the feast, as David's mouth watered in anticipation.

A variety of bottles of soft drink were stacked below the table and just beyond them, half hidden was a stack of beer bottles and several bottles of whisky.

'Leave that alone!' chided an old man, as Malky helped himself to a bottle of beer. 'These can wait until the children have gone to bed.' The old man's tone was affectionate, but his demeanour suggested that he was of some importance. So important in fact that he was able to ignore his own instructions and drink noisily from a pint sized bottle of beer.

Malky was unchastened and still smiling broadly. 'Meet my granda,' he smiled to Helen and David. 'Auld Malk'.

Malky explained that what was about to happen was fairly typical when a boat was to be replaced by a newer model, in this case "Mary-Belle V". The owners, family, friends and neighbours would gather for an almighty party, during which nice things would be said about the old boat

70

before she was set alight. Her "health" might be toasted far into the night.

Tonight's ceremony would be slightly different, in that on Auld Malk's insistence, it would start early, before darkness fell. The heavier drinking would be postponed until after the young children went to bed.

'Granda says this is an important moment in a fishing family's life,' explained Malky, 'and he disnae want the youngsters to miss out. After all they'll be grown up and maybe even left the fishin' afore this ever happens again.'

A middle-aged man who looked as if he might have been Malky's father, produced a gallon can of petrol, and drinks had suddenly appeared in everyone's hands. Everyone was ordered to stand well back.

'Mary-Belle IV' he shouted. 'A fine craft! God bless her and all that ever sailed in her!'

'God bless her!' replied some thirty voices in more or less unison. The man doused the bonfire generously in petrol and threw on a burning match. "Mary-Belle IV's" last voyage had begun.

David and Helen ate their fill and drank generous helpings of the soft drink as it was offered. Elsewhere, Auld Malk's plan to keep the beer and whisky back until the children were in bed was slowly being ignored and the noise levels were increasing considerably. Big Malk, produced a guitar, and perching himself on an upturned barrel, more or less in the centre of things, struck up a few chords. The crowd roared its encouragement.

Oh, I love the sea,
I love the navy,
I love my biscuits
Soaked in gravy.

But, pretty little Black-eyed Susie
My, pretty little Black-eyed Susie
Cross my heart,
I love you best of all!

****

'Fit have yi' deen to my dochter? Faur is she? Yi' bunch o' tinks. I'll kill ivry last one o' yi' if onthing has happened ti'her!'

An irate, distraught and increasing irrational, Erchie Sutherland, had burst into the circle, making as if to knock Big Malk from his barrel. A nearby fisherman leapt to his feet, suddenly grasping his beer bottle by the neck.

For the first time, David became aware of his grandfather and Willie Grant, the village policeman, edging their way into the circle.

'Calm down, Mr Sutherland.' Ordered the policeman, he being the perfect embodiment of calmness, 'I'm sure, there must be a perfectly innocent explanation.' It looked, however, as if Erchie would have to be dragged away from the confrontation.

Auld Malk, had limped slowly to centre stage. Despite, or perhaps because of, his great age, he clearly commanded a great deal of respect.

'It's, okay, Constable,' he said, his hands outstretched like a medieval prophet. ' My grandson invited his two friends here,' he continued, indicating to David and Helen. 'Perhaps we should have been more careful in checking that they had your permission, but I think they have had the time of their lives. Nothing is as important to me as the children. It is an orderly celebration and they are absolutely safe. I apologise for your distress.'

David had rushed to his grandfather's side as soon as he had seen him, and was now snuggled into the rear of his trouser leg, unsure of what he had done wrong and desperately embarrassed that he had caused trouble to his new found friends. Helen had moved more slowly to her father's side, but her presence there now, had drawn Erchie's attention away from Big Malk.

'Would any of you gentlemen like to join us in a drink?' continued the old man.

Davy and Erchie declined.

'Just keep the cork on, Mr Munroe,' said P.C. Grant. 'I'll take it home with me.'

He slid the bottle into the pocket in his trousers specially made for his baton. It fitted perfectly. Then truncheon in hand, he escorted, adults and children from the party.

The afternoon was slowly coming to an end and both David and Helen were aware that teatime was approaching. They had puddled and fished their way well down stream as they talked and merely enjoyed each other's company. They had reached the road leading to the Johnstones' croft but decided to make a detour to reach home by passing old Mrs Hamilton's hovel.

'Look what I see,' yelled Helen as she and Shada raced to the old cottage. David was hard on their heels. 'Weeding!' she gasped, incredulously.

Someone had made a half-hearted attempt to pull out some of the decades' old weeds in what had once been her front garden!

- 10 -

In Demand

Davy did not remember Peem's visit that Wednesday night and remembered little of the early spring. His lung had been punctured. The jar on the floor and the tube to his chest were meant to reinflate it, and they possibly did. But his breathing worsened. The pain from his leg was intense and the healing process slow. It was clear that his leg would be deformed and that Davy would walk with a permanent limp.

Many of his fellow patients would never walk again. It took Davy a long time to realise that he was one of the few civilians on the ward. And the most able bodied.

In that hospital ward Davy got to hear of trenches and lice, mud the likes of which had never been seen in Aberdeenshire and a dark feeling of foreboding, which suggested, that just maybe, there was a whole lot more still to come.

His injured chest meant that his breathing was shallow; his shallow breathing meant that he couldn't expectorate or clear his lungs. His congested lungs encouraged infection and with infection came intermittent delirium.

On the thirty first of March, Davy fought his major battle. As the "nurse", an unhealthy looking lass of about fourteen came to give him his evening meal, a bowl of gruel made from oatmeal and skimmed milk, she sensed that he was "burning up". 'We should maybe tak' his temperature,' said Madge, the "nurse" in charge who six months ago had been caring for her father's pigs. 'Dae you mind nippin' across to Belgium for a thermometer, because I'm damned if yi'll find one at this side o' the watter.'

There was no thermometer, but Iris, the fourteen year old, stayed with him all night, encouraging him to drink and

74

periodically washing him down with cool water from a bucket, using torn up strips of sheets as a flannel.

Davy, who knows what he was thinking, fought her and his demons, all night long. Sometimes he would curse, uncharacteristically, like a trooper, sometimes, despite his state of nakedness, he would struggle to get out of bed, and sometimes he would cry like a baby.

But mercifully, Iris had a helper. Edward, who had lost both eyes on his nineteenth birthday, three months earlier, also stayed up that night. By an unbelievably cruel quirk of fate he could still see when he was dreaming and the "sight" of his pals in the trenches meant that he would rather be awake.

And blind Edward it was, who unseeingly held Davy on his bed. Edward it was too, who slipped his jacket over Iris when, hours after she should have gone home, she dozed briefly on the chair by Davy's bed. The tenderness he showed and the compassion he demonstrated would stay with Davy for life, as, from time to time he recalled the giant steelworker with the touch of a nurse, who horrendously robbed of practically all that was good, had guided him through his longest night.

It was never quite as bad again for Davy although the delirium would come and go for several weeks.

'Madge,' he said one morning, 'I thocht I was deid and in hivven. I could sweir I heard an angel playing "Cock o' the North" on the pipes!'

Madge laughed and her reply was less than complimentary. 'Yi daft gowk. That wisnae heaven, it was right here. Yi might be richt enough aboot the angel though. Yi were listening to oor very ain hero, Piper Findlater, V.C.!'

Davy had first heard about Piper Findlater V.C. when he was a boy. An unassuming, country lad, George Findlater had joined the Gordon Highlanders and seen service in India in 1897. Badly wounded, and under constant enemy fire he, had continued to play his pipes and inspired his colleagues to victory. He was described as 'the most modest recipient of the Victoria Cross, ever.'

Now forty two and a farmer near Turriff in Aberdeenshire, there was no way that George Findlater would be called to fight yet again, but like countless others, he quickly enlisted. Soon, he would be on his way to France, and an uncertain future, but nevertheless, he had taken time out to entertain his injured colleagues with a few rousing pipe tunes.

'Peety I slept through it.' moaned Davy.

Slowly, Iris, Edward and Davy formed a team. The half-fed girl, the blind youth and the mangled would be recruit found their skills complemented each other perfectly and an increasing amount of the ward work began to fall upon their ill-assorted shoulders,

Iris and Davy fed the more helpless patients their food and made their beds. Davy and Edward, carried away the containers of foul smelling urine, and Edward, on Davy's instructions, lifted the laundry, the patients, and with his earthy sense of humour, the spirits of everyone in that desperate place.

Towards the end of summer, Matron, asked to see Davy.

'You'll be ready to go home soon, Mr Gordon,' she began, 'and the doctor tells me that you will never be passed fit to enlist.' She paused long enough to see the disappointment register on his face. 'I thought you might have seen enough in this place to be quite grateful for that, but you and I don't have to go to France to serve the cause. I've been watching you in here, Davy,' she continued, dropping the "Mr Gordon" as they both relaxed, 'and I think you may have found your niche. Billy Stevenson from next door has joined up, although his sister walked all the way from Alford to plead with me to tell the authorities that he was only sixteen, but what can I do? Billy swears he will be nineteen in November.

My main priority, however is to fill the vacant post and ideally, I would like to give it to someone who will be here for the duration of this terrible business. And someone who knows what they are doing! By my reckoning, Davy, you fit both categories.'

'Don't say anything just now,' she said, raising her hand as Davy started to open his mouth. 'I am offering you a full time job as a medical orderly.' She dropped her voice instinctively. 'In this climate, a nurse in everything but name. Food and accommodation are part of the deal, nothing fancy, but as good as anything else out there. The money's not good, but I understand that you are a farm servant, Davy. You won't have been used to a lot.'

Davy was taken aback. And yet he sensed that Matron was probably right. Despite the terrible things he was seeing on a daily basis he felt that, with Iris and Edward, he was making a difference. Now that he thought about it, in a way that was hard to explain, he was actually enjoying himself; and yes, he was good at what he was doing.

Could there possibly be a life for Davy that did not involve frozen turnips, rain sodden fields and bad tempered farmers? None of the male members of his family had ever worked indoors nor had they taken instructions from a female boss. But then none of them had ever bettered themselves either. Davy was tempted. Davy was seriously tempted.

****

But then he had a visitor. Perhaps it was delirium that caused him to forget the few previous visitors who had managed to make the difficult journey to see him, but this time there was no mistake. The dark-haired young woman was definitely looking for him even although he couldn't quite place her vaguely familiar face.

'You and you're fancy ideas!' she blurted out in way of a greeting. 'I see you've landed on your feet.'

She could contain herself no longer, however, and in her haste to receive an answer, the hint of malice was dropped from her voice.

'Oh Davy,' she sobbed. 'Have you heard from your Peem?' Her next question, however, was for her, the most important, 'or my Robbie? Oh Davy, - what's happening ower there?'

77

It was Elsie Cunningham, Robbie Greenhowe's fiancé!

Edward, who had almost mastered the art of walking with a nearly white stick, slowly felt his way forward. 'Would you like a cup of tea?' he asked politely. 'It's our special brand; twenty-five per cent from Ceylon, seventy-five from the joiner's floor across the street. Its disgusting,' he smiled, trying to screw up his already distorted face in what he thought was an appropriate gesture, 'but hot and wet.'

Elsie hoped that her initial urge to recoil from this friendly young man could not be sensed through his makeshift stick or sightless eyes. 'That would be lovely,' she replied. 'Is there anywhere private we could go to drink it, Davy? We've got a lot of talking to do.'

Elsie's eager questions forced Davy to focus on the war in a way that he guiltily realised he hadn't done for some time.

At first, when he had gained some control over his faculties, he had thought a lot about his brother and his pals, mostly bemoaning the fact that he had been robbed of the opportunity to put his grand plan into action and go with them to France. He had heard once from Peem, saying he had completed his basic training somewhere in Perthshire and was on the way south to embark on a troopship. He assumed their parents were probably in regular communication with him.

Elsie had fared little better. Apart from a presumably identical card from Perthshire, she had received one standard format 'field' postcard from somewhere in France. On one side was a caricature of a British soldier that was neither realistic nor humorous, and on the other side, a censor approved couple of sentences saying he was in good health and spirits. Anything else, she assumed, would jeopardise the grand military plan.

Davy decided that Elsie would not normally be an emotional or uptight person, but clearly the war was taking its toll on them all.

'Oh, Davy.' she sobbed. 'What, if he comes here? What if he ends up like that,' she tried to think of a sufficiently horrific word, but had the good grace to correct herself. 'Like your new pal. What if he's worse? What if he disnae ......Oh, Davy, you would tell me wouldn't you?'

She was now sobbing quite uncontrollably and Davy decided she was really quite beautiful and lucky if she was seventeen. He offered her his slightly used handkerchief to wipe her tears.

Davy decided he would tell her about the sudden change in his life plan. Her sudden unexpected appearance had meant he had been unable to share it with those it would affect most; Iris and Edward, but he could keep it to himself no longer.

Elsie got in first.

'There was another reason I came to visit today, Davy.' she said. 'Have you ever heard o' a place ca'd Balcrannie?'

Davy thought that he maybe had. He also thought it was on the coast, stuck somewhere between Aberdeen and Buchan and perhaps, he remembered, there was an old quarry there. It was a place that he had never visited and he was in no great hurry to go back.

Elsie had an uncle, Peter Byers who was in complete charge of a large estate in the parish of Balcrannie and he had to look after it and make it productive while the laird and two thirds of his staff was in the army.

Mr Byers was looking for someone who would stay for the duration of this terrible business, and someone who knew what he was doing. Davy was in demand!

Davy would never be a medical orderly, although he would often wonder, 'what if?' He took his leave a few days later, bound for Balcrannie.

Matron was bitterly disappointed. The patients whose lives he had touched lined up on their wheelchairs and by their beds to give him a rousing farewell. Iris and Edward stood in the background, disconsolate. Tears run down Iris's face, and Edward, lacking the facilities to cry, reached out for her hand.

Davy learned that Edward and Iris got married about four years later. In 1954 he read about their thirty-fifth anniversary in the "Sunday Post".

They had spent their married life across the Dee, next to Craiginches Prison. Iris was in charge of school dinners

- 11 -

Hare Today

That Wednesday evening had taken a long time in coming, but now as the clock slowly ticked towards seven o'clock, David was standing at the crossroads. The bus would be due at any minute.

If he had been less excited about the undoubted adventure ahead he might have felt a little guilty about the subterfuge he had to apply to actually get there. To Helen, he had said that he had to help his grandfather repair a fence at the far end of the field, while to his grandparents, he explained that Mrs Johnstone wanted an update on the duck eggs. To an astounded Shada, it had been, 'Not tonight girl.' as he quickly shut the croft house door.

As far as David understood, the bus was likely to be empty. The earlier bus that passed the crossroads at six o'clock took most of the workers home from their day's toil in Aberdeen. Only those who finished somewhat later caught the seven o'clock bus in which David had enjoyed several free rides in the past.

When it arrived, remarkably close to its correct time, it seemed to be heaving at its seams. In the seat nearest to Sandy, (the seat in which David usually sat) sat a man in his late twenties whose face looked familiar. 'Meet Tosh, the brither.' said Sandy, making no attempt to say who David was. Then for the benefit of the other two passengers he made an exaggerated show of issuing David with an imaginary ticket for his imaginary money,

'Jist in case they're frae the KGB!' he winked.

Tosh was younger than Sandy, taller and a good deal thinner, but nevertheless there was a distinct family resemblance. He seemed, however to lack Sandy's ever present smile.

By his feet, and making the passageway all but impassable were two unimaginatively named greyhounds,

81

Goldie and Soot. Neither it was safe to assume was in possession of a valid ticket.

'Problems,' whispered Sandy, indicating to the two strangers, seated well apart on either side of the corridor. 'Tonight of all nights.'

'We canna change oor minds noo.' hissed a rather impatient Tosh. 'The captain will be hame the morn and I have no idea when I will get the dogs again.'

Sandy seemed uncertain.

He explained to David that his brother Tosh was a handyman to Captain Leggat, who owned a large estate on the other side of Aberdeen. Part of his duties included "dog sitting" on the rare occasions the captain stayed away overnight.

The plan had seemed foolproof. On Cairnton's upper field, far from any house or outbuilding, Sandy had noticed a number of hares, almost every time he drove past. The seven o'clock bus was usually empty by the time it passed Cairnton, and whatever her other faults, old Mrs Johnstone was famous for her hare soup.

But tonight, the bus was not empty.

About three seats behind Tosh, sat an elderly lady who would have looked much more at home sipping coffee in an up market department store in Edinburgh's Princes Street. Above her tweed skirt, she wore a matching twin set while an elaborate and slightly oversized hat was perched at an unusual angle on her head. David's eyes, however, had come to rest on the ample fur stole draped around her neck and his thoughts went back to the "electric hare" at the racetrack! Mercifully, Goldie and Soot did not make the connection.

'A' mothballs and cheap sherry,' whispered Sandy. 'I thocht I wid have to get my gas mask on before I could sell her the ticket!'

On the other side of the corridor, almost at the back of the bus sat a man in his thirties. He wore a well-used dark suit above a pale shirt and red tie. His dark hair was well slicked back with hair cream and the faintest hint of a smile on his sallow face gave the impression that he was watching carefully. And understanding.

The bus was fast approaching Cairnton, and clearly, no one was getting off. Sandy's brow was visibly furrowed; Goldie and Soot seemed to sense that their hour had come.

Tosh and David stared at Sandy, both willing different things. Tosh was determined he should stop; David just wanted to go home. The stranger at the back leant slightly forward in his seat, as if he too, wondered what Sandy would do next.

Sandy stopped. He pulled the bus into what appeared to be a gate into one of the fields, thus allowing just about enough space for any other vehicles to pass in either direction. As before, at least two hares could be seen in the distance, lying stationary, or "flapped" in the long grass.

'Why have we stopped?' demanded the elderly woman, whom David had privately christened "Mrs Jenners" after Edinburgh's premiere store. 'I heve a doctor's appointment, in heff an hour, and eny delay could be catastrophic,' she whined. 'Come on, young man, push, push!'

'There canna be much wrang wi' her if she can mak a noise like that.' Tosh remarked in a voice loud enough to be overheard.

The illogicality of his remarks seemed to further inflame "Mrs Jenners". 'Hurry up young man!' she insisted. 'Does your employers know about these irregularities?'

'I dinna ken fit you need wi' a doctor, onywye,' continued Tosh. 'My mither always said 'Tak an aspirin, when your in pain, rub in lle if your feelin' stiff, sterve a fever an' feed a cauld, and she lived till she deid!'

'Quite the little witch doctor,' reiterated Mrs Jenners, 'I cen see where you got your cherm, but I'm sure your mother didn't have my beck.'

'I'm sure she didna have yir hat either.' muttered Tosh as he turned the handle marked "For Use in Emergencies Only." and escorted Goldie and Soot from the bus.

Sandy seemed unusually flustered. It was his natural instinct to try and keep his customers happy, and besides it was

83

his job on the line if "Mrs Jenners" should decide to make an official complaint.

'A call of nature,' he explained, indicating towards the greyhounds. 'Their bladders.' he continued delicately.

The stranger at the back of the bus spoke for the first time. 'I hope its not her bladder that's taken this lady here to see her doctor, Sandy,' he grinned. 'Unless you've got a spare bucket somewhere on your bus!'

David cringed with embarrassment. "Mrs Jenners" made a great show of her indignation and wrapping her stole even more tightly round her neck, managed to turn her back on everyone.

And then, despite her best intentions, her eyes were drawn to the antics of Tosh and his borrowed dogs.

Tosh had, with some difficulty, kept the two dogs on their leads, and in a semi crouched position was making his way towards the top of the distant field, behind the cover of the dry stone dyke that marked its boundary. His plan was to encircle the unsuspecting hares emerging from the dry stone dyke at a point beyond them. This meant that the dogs would have the whole length of the field in which to pursue their quarry and that all would be running in the direction of the bus.

'Eh'll give you one more minute, young man.' declaimed "Mrs Jenners". 'Hev you any idea what a doctor's appointment would cost me in Fleet Street?' she asked.

'Harley Street,' David corrected her silently, 'and how irrelevant could a question be?' when suddenly the old woman continued. 'Michtie me,' she proclaimed. 'Fit are they manky beasts deeing?'

Tosh had climbed the dry stane dyke and was just visible at the very top of the field. He had just released the two dogs, and a hare, immediately alert, shot from the grass apparently already in full flight.

'Utterly outrageous! ' Shrieked "Mrs Jenners," regaining her "posh" accent. 'Eh demand to be teken to the nearest telephone booth. You will never drive a bus again!'

The stranger had crossed the passageway, and was now pressed hard against the window, watching intently as the three animals zigzagged across the field in what, for the hare at least, was a life or death mission. 'I'll have five bob on the black dog, Sandy,' he appeared to joke.

"Mrs Jenners'" demeanour changed immediately. 'Are we allowed to bet on the outcome?' she shrieked. 'How thrilling! I take it you are the bookmaker, Sendy?' she continued, rifling through her ancient purse. 'Eh'll have ten shillings on the hare getting clean away!' As if on cue, the hare veered suddenly for the umpteenth time and shooting off in the opposite direction gained a few extra yards on the greyhounds who were forced to turn more ponderously. 'Make that twelve and sixpence, Sendy!' she shouted.

Two thunderous blasts rent the air almost simultaneously. The greyhounds slithered to a confused halt. Yet again, David longed to be anywhere rather than in the centre of this mess and the hare skipped gratefully, clean away.

A furious, round looking man with a red face and wearing the ridiculous plus fours favoured by the gentry stood only a few yards in front of the bus. He clutched his still smoking shotgun with both hands, its butt on the ground in front of him, the barrels pointing to the sky at which he had fired his warning shots.

Sandy, still sitting firmly in the driver's seat, seemed remarkably unruffled.

'Well, well, Stanley,' he grinned to the figure with the gun, 'I see yi' hivnae learned to sheet ony straighter yet. My wife was just saying the ither day, that she could be deein' wi' a brace o' spitfires if yi' bring them doon accidentally. Apparently they mak afa' fine soup!'

'Sandy Stronach,' the strange man blustered. 'I am the gamekeeper on this estate and once again you have put me in an impossible position. Have you any idea how many laws you have broken with this nonsense?' he demanded. 'Trespass, poaching, illegal parking, not to mention doing them at a time when you are drawing wages from your employer. That amounts to theft in my book.'

Tosh, who had retaken his seat in the bus, whispered to the stranger who had now given up his seat at the back and moved nearer to everyone else, 'Nae to mention illegal gambling and corrupting a minor.'

The gamekeeper was still in full flight. 'The jails in this country, are full of more honourable men than you Sandy.' he lectured, then just as David started to sob, he split his shotgun in half, clicked his heels and started to walk away.

'Good day,' he said officiously, and then, more quietly, 'give my regards to Doreen.'

David was entirely perplexed by this sudden change of attitude from the gamekeeper. At one moment they all seemed destined for jail, and the next, they seemed to be off the hook. His eager questions brought a short response from Sandy.

'Brithers at arms,' he confided. 'We were brithers at arms.'

"Mrs Jenners" had been silent for all of two minutes.

'What a thrilling adventure, Sendy. Can I have my twelve and sixpence now? You know, I feel ever so much better. I think I can forget all about seeing that doctor. Oil, you said Mr Stronach?' she addressed Tosh whilst rubbing her back. 'Do you happen to know which variety?'

- 12 -

Cat Burglars

David often wondered if he was the only person among his acquaintances who was interested in politics. It was clear to him that a general election was going to be called in the near future, yet no one seemed to care. David understood that he was part of the free world and that more than half the world did not share this favoured status.

As he understood it a large part of the world was governed by a communist system, which allowed no elections, and which threatened the very existence of modern life, as it was understood in Great Britain. From his reading of the situation it seemed at least some communists wanted to spread their politics across the globe and to use their atom bombs on anyone who disagreed with them. As far as he could tell, the free world, which he understood to be Great Britain and America along with a few allies of varying reliability also had these bombs but were far too gentlemanly to use them unless they were fired on first.

In the four minutes or so left between the bombs being fired at them and the total destruction of civilisation, David understood, the free world might retaliate.

After all these foreign chaps would need to be taught a lesson and would have to realise that they couldn't go around destroying civilisation as we know it without getting a jolly thick lip in return.

David could not understand why, if half the world were prepared to die for the vote that was denied them, the other half was more interested in housey housey and the hula hoop than in the forthcoming election. Whenever it might be called.

To make matters even more puzzling it seemed to David that here as in nothing else his two identities, that is, the Edinburgh David and the Balcrannie David seemed worlds apart.

The Edinburgh Leith constituency to which he belonged appeared to elect Labour candidates all the time. Mr J. H. Hoy the local Member of Parliament whom David had once seen entering the Boundary Bar would, according to Peggy almost definitely be re-elected at any forthcoming election. David was unsure how active his mother was in politics but felt certain that she would be happy if this took place.

'Labour stands for the working man, and more importantly, the working woman,' she had once explained. 'Without Labour, we would never have had a National Health Service,' she continued, 'and our NHS is the envy of the world. Ask any American, Japanese or Russian that you like and they will tell you.'

Not knowing any Americans, Japanese or Russians, David decided to take her word for it. After all, the NHS paid his mother's wages and they were getting by.

But herein lay the mystery. As far as David could tell, no one worked as hard as his grandfather who was out in all weathers, lifting huge sacks of potatoes or corn, or up to his elbows in mud as he struggled with the croft's inadequate drainage system. His granny too, toiled incessantly outdoors in the fields and in the house that was totally lacking in anything that resembled a modern convenience.

Yet in their eyes, the Labour Party, or Socialists as they usually called it, was all that was bad!

'They canna handle the money!' Granda had stated emphatically on a rare occasion that he talked politics. 'Ivry Socialist government there's iver been has left the country bankrupt. Fit dae yi' expect? They should leave that kind o' thing tae them wi' the experience tae handle it.'

He spoke as if everything he said was a self-evident fact that brooks no argument. He was the wisest person that David had ever met and he had never before known his judgement to be faulty. David was confused.

West Aberdeenshire, in which lay the parish of Balcrannie, had never returned a Labour or Socialist member of parliament to Westminster.

David had been pondering on this thorny issue as he tended Alma and her duck eggs. They were now almost three weeks into the project, and all but one of the eggs were intact. Alma had accidentally broken one and David had been astounded to see the perfectly formed features of a tiny, lifeless, duckling amongst the eggshells. Life as a duck owner clearly beckoned!

David had often stood at the junction of Leith Walk and the beginning of London Road, only yards from his home and contemplated what life would be like in London, almost three hundred and fifty miles away in the completely opposite direction from Balcrannie.

'Was it totally outrageous?' he sometimes asked himself. 'To think that one day, he, David Gordon, crofter's grandson, could be an M.P. in the so called "Mother of Parliaments".' Considering the opposing messages he got from his loved ones, he concluded, it probably was.

David was still thinking politics as he met up with Helen on the road to Mrs Hamilton's for what he felt sure was going to be an ill-advised liaison.

'Whom would you vote for?' he asked,' if we had the chance?'

Helen had obviously given the matter a great deal of thought.

'Elvis Presley, in all categories,' she immediately replied, 'except for the best British singer, of course. That would be Cliff, but I dinna think he's got half the sex appeal o' Elvis. What do you think, David?'

David groaned inwardly. The polls that were exciting Helen had nothing to do with the all-important upcoming election, but were being conducted by something called "The New Musical Express," a publication that David had never read. As for sex appeal, he wasn't sure exactly what it meant, but vaguely thought it may be something to do with Helen's changing appearance and the fact that he couldn't see enough of her, even though they seemed to have much less in common than in years gone by.

But tonight, they had business to attend to.

'I see you got the bags.' Helen smiled approvingly. 'Now a' we have to do is fill them!'

David had taken three large hessian sacks from his Grandfather's potato shed as instructed and Helen seemed pleased. Each sack was made to hold one hundredweight of potatoes, but tonight, their contents would be very much different.

'Are you sure this is a good idea?' asked David. 'I mean, do you really think it will work?'

Helen seemed less than pleased that she was being questioned, but tried to be patient.

'Think aboot it, David,' she insisted. 'Ever since we started taking an interest in this auld witch, her place has been hoaching wi' cats, I've seen twenty or thirty of them here at one time. Now there doon ti' single figures! She's droonin' them, David. We've got to save the one's that are left, especially the kittlins.'

David was uncertain. The number of cats laying claim to Mrs Hamilton's cottage had certainly diminished and much as though he hated to think about it, he knew that drowning kittens or kittlins as they were usually called was a well-established way of keeping numbers down amongst country people. He had once asked his grandfather about it.

'They say if you get them young enough, before they're een are open and before they can survive on their ain, it disnae hurt them. Bit I widnae di it mysel'.'

As far as tonight's venture was concerned, Helen made it sound very straightforward. They would simply hide as close to the house as possible and grab any passing cat, whatever its age, and if they still had room in their sacks they may even enter the old outhouse which various clans of felines seemed to regard as their headquarters. With their sacks bulging with grateful pussies it would simply be a case of implementing plan "B".

Perhaps this would be a good time to tell Helen that there was no plan "B". It had sounded perfectly straightforward. Helen had instructed David to enrol the help of Sandy Stronach, and more importantly, his bus. Once the cats were

90

literally in the bag, they could be smuggled aboard Sandy's bus as he was making his way to Aberdeen. Once he had got rid of his passengers, Sandy could simply empty the sacks into the streets, where Helen was certain, hundreds of children would be desperate to give a free cat a good home. Just in case there were more cats than prospective owners, Helen suggested that they be freed in the harbour area of the town where any enterprising feline could scrape a living from stolen fish and dozy pigeons.

But David had not had the opportunity to ask Sandy for his cooperation and could feel things going very badly wrong. Granda's shed, he feared might have to provide temporary accommodation to the grateful escapees.

After half an hour things had not gone according to plan. No cat had approached either Helen or David, which considering their half wild state seemed scarcely surprising. But worse, any attempt to spring from cover and "ambush" a passing cat, resulted in bared claws, frenzied spitting and the beating of a hasty retreat often accompanied by the screech of a sympathetic chicken.

'It will soon be dark,' hissed Helen. 'It will be a piece of cake then.' she assured David, ignoring the fact that cats can see in the dark and they most definitely could not.

Ten minutes later, and still catless, the duo decided that they must be more active. With scarcely a glance towards the blacked out windows of the cottage, they darted towards the outhouse. There was a fastening on the door, but despite the rapidly falling darkness, David quickly discovered how it worked. They exchanged a silent "thumbs up" and sacks at the ready, slipped into the outhouse!

It was dark, and very scary. As he grew accustomed to the darkness, David grabbed at the cat behind the large pair of eyes staring down at him from what he assumed to be a shelf or piece of discarded household furniture. He was rewarded with a vicious snarl and a scratching attack that drew blood from the entire length of his arm. Helen grabbed a "kitten" only to discover that it was covered in feathers and determined to remain "ungrabbed".

91

Cats and hens clearly lived in harmony in this hellhole and neither wished to be rescued. It was time to admit defeat and go home. Then it happened.

A loud clang and some slight movement from the direction of the door could mean only one thing. It had been fastened from the outside!

They were at the mercy of the Auld Witch!

David was frightened. He didn't really believe in witches and probably thought that Mrs Hamilton, was eccentric, lonely and despite his mother's protestations to the contrary, possibly mentally ill.

Helen's superior and more outrageous imagination, for once, did not act in her favour. She believed everything they had ever said about Mrs Hamilton and accepted that they were now at the mercy of supernatural forces. David was more worried about the likely reactions of P.C. Willie Grant, his grandparents and if ever she got to hear about it, his mother. His next comment proved highly unhelpful.

'Was Gretel, the boy or the girl?' he asked innocently, and for the first time in their long relationship, Helen burst unashamedly into tears.

Although city born and bred, David was familiar with country ways and had the resourcefulness of someone used to fending for himself. He knew that cats or hens could not go through a door that was usually closed and that somewhere near the floor there must be a "pop-hole" or cat flap.

As Helen wept hysterically, he quickly located it, in what was, after all, a smallish shed. The original hole was too small to allow a human to pass, but the shed had been simply constructed half a lifetime ago and neglected ever since. With one well-placed kick, the timber surrounding the pop-hole shattered. They could escape!

Quickly he dragged Helen to the hole, and having firstly slipped through himself, he pulled her through to safety. There troubles were over!

But not quite and not so fast. Too late, David saw a light shining from the open cottage door, and seconds later he heard the sound of a shotgun being discharged skywards for the second time in a fortnight!

Having a qualified gamekeeper firing a shot over your head is one thing, but a mad witch, for David had changed his mind again and now truly believed that was what she was, was a different matter altogether. They ran as they had never ran before, until finally, hearts pounding they collapsed behind a hedge some half a mile from the scene of their crime.

'What is it with you Balcrannie folk?' gasped David, forgetting that unlike the villagers, the farms and their cottages had still to be attached to the electricity grid. 'Do you all think you're Bronco Lane?'

Helen looked vague. 'Whose Bronco Lane?' she asked.

- 13 -

Home and Away

Davy Gordon forced himself awake as his alarm clock, which had cost him the best part of a week's wages, thundered incessantly in the background. It was the summer of 1916 and he had been working on the Balcrannie Estate for the best part of a year.

His injuries were as well as they would ever be and his pain more than bearable. He was lucky.

The work on the estate was lighter than on the farm, and with no animals to attend to, his day started at seven with breakfast in the kitchen of the big house. Normally his working day would be finished by six. Yet Davy was disgruntled.

For weeks now he had been engaged in singling turnips or as it was known locally hoeing or "hyowing" neeps. Turnips were central to the northeast farm, providing essential winter feeding for the animals and playing a vital part in the rotation of crops. Grass, oats, potatoes and turnips would be grown in different fields each year in a carefully managed order, which allowed the soil to remain fertile and productive indefinitely.

But the production and harvesting of turnips was highly labour intensive. The turnip seeds were sown liberally in long lines or drills in the spring and spent their first few weeks fighting with their neighbours and a huge amount of perennial weeds, for their very existence. Then the hoeing would begin.

A hoe consisted of a blade like contraption about eight inches in length and set at right angles to a long handle or shaft which was held in both hands by the operator. The "singling" consisted with every stroke of the hoe, of removing all but one miniature turnip which would then have ample room to grow to maturity. At the same time, pushing them from the soil destroyed the masses of potentially murdering weeds. Without hoeing, the turnips would die en masse, crowded out by their fellow seedlings and suffocated by the ever-present weeds.

Once the art of hoeing was mastered, it could be performed swiftly, which was fortunate, since every inch of every turnip field had to be covered in a relatively short space of time. It was common for women and every available non-farm servant in the vicinity to be employed in this task and work frequently continued until dusk. It was monotonous, back breaking and depending on the weather, liable to produce sunburn or rheumatism.

As this day dawned, Davy bemoaned the fact that it was going to be just like yesterday, and tomorrow, he guessed, would be exactly the same.

He wished he were in France.

Robbie and Tam had not slept that night. After a fortnight in the frontline trench, they might have been hoping for some relief, the long slow retreat to take up a reserve position perhaps half a mile from the action. Or just occasionally, a week or so of rest and recuperation with the chance of a proper wash and a bottle of beer. Maybe even some female company.

But for a day or two now, they knew that this time was different. And today was the day.

The big guns had roared as always, but as dawn threatened to break, the noise rose to a deafening crescendo and the vibrations made the compulsory wet shave almost impossible. A chap could do himself a serious mischief while shaving!

The padre had visited and a tot of rum was issued. At 08.00 hours with the 9th Devons on their left, the Gordon Highlanders would attack. They were somewhere on the Somme and their objective was the village of Mametz.

It was fitting that Tam and Robbie should go over the top together. They had been together in every flea-infested trench, every corpse-strewn mud bath since that morning they had left the station at Inverurie to enlist. They had been together as they grew relentlessly thinner from the effects of putrid rations and infected water, while the rats, their constant companions, grew fat on the flesh of their fallen companions.

They saw Peem on a daily basis and Wullie, who had found himself in catering, a little less regularly. They spoke of New Zealand only rarely now and dreamt merely of their survival. All would be in action today.

With two minutes to go, final orders were re-issued. The incessant bombardment of the last few days would mean that the Germans' barbed wire defences would be destroyed, and the enemy would be dead, demoralised or deserted. They were to march purposefully rather than run towards the enemy, as this was calculated to instil greater fear in any straggling Germans still at their post.

The whistle blew, and the terrified mismatch of clerks, labourers and farm servants charged, some running some marching and many falling over. The barbwire had not been destroyed and the enemy had not fled. Instead they commanded the high ground and the deadliest of machine guns.

The slaughter was complete. Many Scots were mowed down by machine gun fire within yards of their own trenches. As many more were butchered on the barbed wire, like fish caught in a net. No military advantage was gained.

To this day the Gordon Cemetery marks the spot where 102 men of the Gordon Highlanders lie buried in a huge shell hole.

Left on the battlefield that day, were the corpses of Privates Thomas Simpson, Alexander "Peem" Gordon, and Lance Corporal Robert Greenhowe.

And half of Private Wullie Reid's face.

-14 -

All Hands on Deck

If David thought he could slip quietly into the croft house undetected, following his latest shotgun incident he was to be disappointed. Despite the lateness of the hour, he was surprised to see Maggie Burnett's car parked outside.

The nurse in her was quick to spot the large scratch marks on his hand and forearm and to inquire about their acquisition.

'He'll have been climbin' trees on that Pirate Ship o' his,' his Granny intervened, and to David, 'I do wish you would stay oot o' trouble when yi'r bidin' here. What would yir mither say if you set your neck and her at the ither end o' the country?'

Maggie had produced a bottle of the stingiest antiseptic known to man and started to apply a totally unnecessary bandage. 'It's a good job that it wisna a cat that did this.' she said. 'Itherwise yi' micht waken in the mornin' a' seized up wi' the lockja'.'

David realised that she was threatening him with paralysis, but tried to look nonchalant. After all, he was feigning innocence.

Suddenly, her tone changed. 'Fit wid yi' say ti' a wireless, loon?' she asked with what could almost have been tenderness in her voice. Never having conversed with a radio before, David was unsure how to reply.

'I've jist bocht a brand new een,' she continued. 'There's nivver been a wireless like it, bit there wis nithin' wrang wi' my auld een. Wid yi'like a present o'it, loon? It should work fine in here without ony aerial or weet batteries.'

David was amazed. He had never owned a radio before and now this comparative stranger appeared to be offering him one free of charge. He was unsure what to say.

'Do you get Radio Luxemburg on it?' he asked quietly.

97

'That you do.' Replied Maggie kindly. 'You young folk are a' the same wi' yir Radio Luxemburg. I nivver listen ti' it misel', bit yi'll be a'right for yir "Top Twinty" noo!'

David had no real interest in the "Top Twenty" or indeed Radio Luxemburg. But he knew someone who had!

'That would be lovely, Nurse Burnett,' he said. 'Thank you very much.'

He was glad to retire to bed with his thoughts. Life had taken an unexpected turn for the better.

'Peer, peer, loon,' he thought he heard Granny saying just as he'd closed the door. How touching that she should be so concerned about a mere scratch.

Granda had a busy day planned for David, and for Tibbie. The first of the peats were sufficiently dried to be carted home and stacked for the winter, and for once, "Fergie" was not required. The old box cart had not been converted for the tractor, so a rare day's work beckoned for Tibbie. David was delighted.

The track to the spot where the peats lay was approximately a quarter of a mile long and skirted on either side by deep banked ditches and the occasional "pot hole", a pond like mass of dark water with a soft and treacherous bottom. The track, itself, was solid, but elsewhere the ground tended to be swampy.

As horse and empty cart made its way to the waiting peats David sat on board, loosely holding the reins, while Shada, uncharacteristically still, snuggled by his side. Granda walked by the horse's head encouraging her with gentle conversation whilst lightly holding her halter.

Once the cart was filled, a job that took about twenty minutes vigorous labour, David and Shada would run ahead, while Granda would lead Tibbie homewards at a pace, which considering their advancing years, suited them both.

By mid afternoon, the journey had been completed some half a dozen times and a considerable amount of winter fuel had been taken home. It had been a hard, satisfying but uneventful day, David had just decided. Then disaster struck.

As Tibbie rounded a corner on to the track, she perhaps cut the corner a little fine. The wheel of the cart struck a sizeable stone that had previously been unobserved, causing it to veer off the track, dragging the unsuspecting Tibbie back with it, onto the swampy ground.

'Quick, David!' shouted Granda with an unprecedented sense of urgency. 'We've laired!'

David knew that "laired" meant sunk in the swamp like ground and ran to assist. Such incidents were an ever-present danger in damp terrain.

The old man and the young boy pushed at the laden cart whilst shouting encouragement to Tibbie in an attempt to get her to pull in unison. But the task was clearly beyond them. Moreover, the position of the cart was such that with every pull, Tibbie, lunged nearer the pothole. She was clearly becoming agitated.

Granda quickly realised that he had to free the horse from the cart, which could be retrieved at any time in the future when more hands were available to help. Quickly he released her from the shafts of the cart and gave her a gentle slap to encourage her to move forward. But the frightened horse was too near the edge of the pothole. As momentarily confused, she stumbled forward, the bank slowly gave way. She was in water, halfway up her legs.

Old Davy could just about reach her halter and tried to drag the massive horse clear, but he was powerless. David could reach nothing but was vaguely aware of yelling encouragement to his dear friend. Shada barked unconvincingly.

'She canna lift her feet,' yelled the now panicking Davy. 'We're going to lose her, David! She's gaun ti' droon!' He was clearly struggling with his emotions, 'Rin, loon, rin!' he yelled at David. ' We need men. Rin ti' the home ferm. We need a tractor, and rope! Oh rin, loon rin!'

David ran.

Mossyhillock may have been remote, but neighbours knew how to rally in an emergency. Within a matter of minutes, three men and a tractor had arrived from Home Farm.

Helen whom David had met by chance was running to the Anderson's farm and right on cue Sandy Stronach rolled up in his bus. It was his free time in the afternoon and once again, he had been using his bus as if it was his private car.

But almost first on the scene was a vaguely familiar stranger with a badly worn dark suit.

The men threw themselves into the challenge as if their lives depended on it as Tibbie's surely did. But it was to no avail. The more the men pulled the more Tibbie stood still, and she was slowly sinking into the quagmire at the bottom of the pool.

We'll have to lift her oot!' said the tractor man from Home Farm. 'But how can we possibly do that?'

The stranger spoke for the first time. 'Give me the rope,' he said in a voice slightly more refined than the others. 'It has to be passed under her belly.'

Tibbie had now sank to such an extent that the water was at least half up her legs and the treacherous mud was only about two feet from her underbelly. She was too far from the side of the hole for anything to be passed under her easily.

The stranger was stripping off his worn suit to reveal a none too clean set of underwear. 'I take it I am the only swimmer, here?' he said and no one attempted to argue. 'I need a tattie bag.' He said authoritively, and then holding two pieces of rope, he dropped into the black water.

David was horrified. He had never heard of anyone voluntarily going into a pothole before and had frequently been warned by all the important adults in his life that to do so was to court almost certain death. Within thirty seconds, however the stranger surfaced, at the other side of Tibbie, spitting out mouthfuls of the repulsively dark water, but still clutching the two ropes. It was then that David noted that Home Farm's tractorman was holding the other ends.

'Stage one completed.' grinned the stranger. 'I see the tattie bag has appeared'.

The "tattie" bag had originally been made to hold one hundredweight of potatoes, and empty, was perhaps a little over three feet long.

'Here we go!' he gasped clutching the bag, and having handed his ropes to a bystander, he once again plunged into the water.

Paddling on his back in the space between Tibbie's underbelly and the quagmire into which she was sinking, the stranger pushed the sack under the two ropes to make almost a sling and a buffer to protect her skin from the ropes when they were pulled tightly.

The stranger emerged from the water and fixed Sandy with his eyes. 'You ken what it's got to be Sandy,' he muttered grimly.

Realisation dawned on Sandy's face. 'The Kwia?' he spluttered, 'and there's no time to waste!'

'Let's go,' he yelled, taking command and punching his permanently gloved right hand in the air. 'We need stakes, plenty of them, and all the rope we can get our hands on and, dear God we need something that will act as a beam!'

Two tractors had already burst into life. 'Hillie's new barn,' yelled the Home Farm tractorman, they're pittin' a new roof on it as we spik! And the corn yards! There'll be stakes there! Come on, Lads. Times rinnin' oot!'

'Bring a few bags o' potatoes, if you can!' shouted the stranger as the tractors lurched off.

Old Davy had slumped to the ground as the first of the helpers arrived. Too broken hearted to think straight, suddenly too frail for the heavy work and frankly, too old to assume the leadership role so easily commandeered by Sandy and the stranger. Only David and Shada sitting at his feet seemed to be paying him much attention.

The tractors had been gone for some ten minutes when Davy sprang to his feet. 'It's too late!' he sobbed, 'She's gaun doon. We've lost her!'

It was obvious that Tibbie was in big trouble. Perhaps because she was being dragged incessantly into the quagmire, perhaps because she had become overcome by inertia, her head was slumping into the water. In a few minutes, she would surely drown.

101

As the helpers returned, the stranger re-entered the water for far his most dangerous mission. Tibbie's head had to be physically held above the water and he had to do it without letting his own feet touch the bottom. If they did, the stranger would surely be dragged under. Paddling on his back, he grabbed the horse's head in what David considered to be a lifeguard type grip and began to tread water.

The other five or six men were working flat out under the direction of Sandy and relying heavily on the rope tying expertise of wee Andy Fife, the orraman, who had spent the war in the Merchant Navy.

Quickly two pyramid shaped contraptions were formed. Consisting of three long poles or stakes used to build corn ricks around or borrowed from the building site at the barn, and roped together at the top, they looked for all the world like a Red Indian's tepee, without any coverings.

Now came the tricky part, with a "tepee" placed on either side of the pot hole, the final beam had to be placed on top to form a "goalpost" type contraption, with the "crossbar" passing over the floundering horse. In fact the "crossbar" consisted of two beams borrowed from the new barn and bound tightly together to give added strength. But it still looked decidedly flimsy.

Andy had somehow attached the four rope ends, which had passed under Tibbie to one long rope and at the second attempt flung it over the crossbar. Let "the tug of war" commence.

The men jostled for a place on the rope, and on Sandy's command took the strain. The "crossbar" creaked but for the moment held firm, Tibbie aware of the movement looked round. The stranger wondered how much longer he and Tibbie could stay above water.

The men heaved in unison at Sandy's command, the "crossbar" seemed insufficient for the job, when suddenly but almost imperceptibly, something started to move. A "slurping" noise suggested that Tibbie's feet were extricating themselves from the quagmire.

'The tatties!' yelled the stranger. 'Get them in the watter!'

Only David and his granda were free, but thankfully the old man realised what was required. The two of them half carried, half rolled, the one hundredweight bags to the side of the water and heaved them in at the horse's feet.

'Heave!'

Something was definitely happening. Tibbie's front feet were immerging from the quagmire! Instinctively, she placed one foot on a submerged sack of potatoes, then another. They didn't sink immediately, but allowed her the leverage to extract her hind legs from the mire. She scrambled free!

Sandy was the first to drag the exhausted stranger from the water.

'Who would have thocht these bloody Japs could have taught us onything useful!' he muttered as they hugged each other briefly.

Davy, with David by his side slowly approached the stranger and offered him his hand. 'Thank you Bert,' he said rather tersely. 'I owe you everything. You risked your life for that old horse.'

He turned to David. 'David, I want you to meet Mr Hamilton. Our neighbour, Mrs Hamilton's son.'

David gulped and as his grandfather turned away the stranger leant forward conspiratorially. 'How's your arse for pellets, these days?' he winked.

It all made horrible sense. Bertie Hamilton had been the stranger on the bus on the day they went chasing hares. And Mrs Hamilton had not fired the shots from her cottage door, the previous evening.

15

Living Doll

David had risen early on the day after Tibbie's accident and rushed to reassure himself that all was well. He need not have feared. The old horse greeted him with her usual enthusiasm. Things seemed back to normal.

Granda, however, seemed far from normal and was already in full flight when David joined him and Granny at breakfast.

'Tae think,' he groaned, 'that o' a' the folk that could have saved Tibbie's life, yesterday, it had to be a bloody socialist!'

Granny was clearly not encouraging him.

'From fit you say, Davy,' she chided him. 'It took a very special person to save Tibbie yesterday. In the circumstances, is his politics really important?'

David sensed some excitement.

'Is Mr Hamilton a socialist?' he asked. 'But Helen said that he was in the jail, or,' he hesitated, knowing of his mother's sensitivities, 'or clean aff his heid.'

'Oh, he's that a' right,' replied Granda, 'Although, I dinna ken aboot being in the jile. He's bin somewye since the end o' the war. That's for sure.'

'Mrs Johnstone says he sometimes gets in touch wi' Sandy,' Granny explained. 'He went tae the London School o' Economics when he came back fae the Far East.'

David listened intently but his grandfather was unimpressed.

'An economist! That's jist fit this country needs. Mair economists. Fit wye couldn't he be mair like Sandy and tak' his PSV licence. Yi can niver hae ower mony bus drivers!'

Davy was in full flight, but Granny intervened again. From what she had heard, Bertie Hamilton was not an economist, but a politician. If Mrs Johnstone could be believed, that was why he was back in the parish after some eighteen years. It seemed that a general election was imminent and Bertie, an experienced election agent, had been sent by the Labour Party to organise their campaign in what was, for them, a hostile environment.

It would be a hard task, but at the last election in 1955 he had worked in a Glasgow constituency and proved himself to be a meticulous organiser and doughty fighter.

'A politician?' gasped Davy. Like most people he knew, he had never met a politician, and that suited him just fine. 'Nae wonder his poor mither became so, - *different*' he muttered, regaining his tact. 'It would mak' onybody ging fair gyte!'

'Surely it was the Far East that did that,' interrupted Granny, 'and anyway, Mrs Hamilton was always a bit, *different.*'

David had just decided that he must pay Bertie Hamilton a visit at the earliest opportunity when Maggie Burnett's car drew up at the door.

'Why don't you two see if you can get this thing going!' she said, placing a sizeable radio into David's outstretched hands.

Spluttering his thanks, David scurried towards his bedroom, his hands full of the cherished "wireless" with his now calm, grandfather at his heels.

'Well, Elsie, foo are yi' the day?' asked Maggie.

As David had expected, Helen was delighted to hear about the radio and after checking if it received Radio Luxemburg her next question was even more eagerly put.

'Dis it hae transistors? Will we be able to cairry it aboot outside?'

David had to disappoint her. From what he understood, Maggie's new purchase had all these properties, but this one would have to stay firmly in his bedroom.

'Its nae fair,' groaned Helen. 'You'll get ti listen ti "Top Twinty" on Sunday nicht and I winna, I'll be a laughin' stock.' She looked every inch the young girl that she had so recently been.

David could not see the problem. Having acquired the radio by a stroke of good fortune, he was more than willing to share it.

'There's no school, on Monday. You can come here and listen to it if you like.' he offered.

And for the first time ever, Helen planted a huge kiss on his forehead.

David had not been particularly interested in the Top Twenty but knew that it was eagerly listened to by many of his classmates, especially those with older brothers and sisters. It was broadcast from eleven p.m. until midnight on a Sunday night and provided much of the small talk amongst teenagers on a Monday morning. The advertising jingles for shampoo and chocolate bars themselves became instantly recognisable and a good deal more durable than most of the songs featured in the programme.

Helen had thought of nothing else but the radio programme since David had invited her to listen to it with him and the week dragged on interminably. However, Sunday finally arrived and by ten forty five, she was, slightly panting, knocking at his bedroom window, her expectations high.

David was pleased to let her in. The door from his room conveniently opened directly outside and thus did away with any need for Helen to walk through the house proper and that is perhaps why he did not tell his grandparents about his plans. They tended not to share his enthusiasm for Helen, simply because they had never bothered to get to know her finer points, he was sure, and anyway they were about to retire to bed.

'Fit dae you think will be number one?' she whispered excitedly.

David could make no suggestion. He really wanted the radio to listen to commentaries on football matches and especially, middle of the night boxing matches from America featuring the likes of the newly crowned heavyweight champion Ingemar Johansson or Floyd Paterson and knew little of pop music. The prospect of an illicit hour of Helen's undivided company, however, seemed more than adequate compensation.

'We'll have to wait and see.' he replied, indicating that she should sit next to him on the bed. The makeshift bedroom was much too small to have any chairs in it.

The rest of the house seemed silent, but they turned down the sound, just in case, and as the programme started David blew out the paraffin lamp.

'We could be the only two folk left in the world,' he giggled as the uninspiring record that was number twenty, screeched in the background.

Helen snuggled closer.

A couple of tunes, that were more to David's taste followed and then for the first time, he actually recognised a number, an instrumental which his mother frequently whistled. It was going 'way down,' according to the announcer.

David wondered how his Mum had been getting on in the month or so that he had been away.

Helen had never been happier. 'It's Elvis!' she shrieked, as "A Fool Such As I," which had earlier been at number one for about a month suddenly came on air. 'He's absolutely terrific!' she screeched.

David had never heard the word "terrific" before but assumed that it meant "pretty special", and if he were to be honest, the Elvis song was far superior to anything else that had been on so far. He decided not to admit as much to Helen, however.

"These Americans should stick to boxing. They're good at that.' he heard himself say and was rewarded with an indignant elbow in the ribs.

David retaliated as he had done so many times before, and with a giggle, grabbed her offending arm and wrestled her flat on the bed. For good measure, he playfully chucked his pillow on her head.

With a noisy chuckle she managed to entwine him with her legs and brought him crashing down on top of her. Quickly she transferred the pillow from her face to his and the two of them laughed once more. But he was not finished with

107

her yet! Quick as a flash, he returned the offending pillow to her face and followed up with the other one to her head. They were on their knees, shrieking, plummeting and laughing.

The music played on.

This was fun! And just like the pillow fights, David had read about in his comic books. The kind, he reasoned he would have had with a brother or a sister if he had not been an only child. But maybe not.

Helen through the bedcover at him and he caught it. Throwing it round his shoulders, he dragged her down again and suddenly they were both exhausted. With the cover on top of them, they wrestled some more, giggled and held each other much more tightly than was comfortable.

David gazed at Helen's face. She was looking as she had never looked before and he desperately wanted to kiss her. But what was Helen thinking, what were her expectations? Somehow he had always imagined that it was she that would know what to do.

****

After two massive thumps, the bedroom door flew open and a bright torch was shone in the startled children's faces. Because if Erchie Sutherland had looked closely that is what he would have seen. Two frightened children.

But the cattleman was mad with fury. So mad that he had turned the knob of the door to open it only after twice having attempted to kick it in. Now the butt of his anger was David.

'You big toon blackguards, wi' yir funcy wyes!' he roared. 'Yi' think yi' can dae whit yi' like wi' country folk like oorsels. Well I'm tellin' you, loon. If you've as much touched a hair o' oor Helen's heid, I'll tak' you outside an' droon yi' in that horse trough and gladly hing for yi'!'

The terrified twelve year old, unsure of what he was supposed to have done, opened his mouth, but no words came. Erchie Sutherland drew back his clenched fist.

'Aaaah!' he bellowed, jumping back and trying to clutch his left ankle. 'Dinna think yi'll get awa' wi' this!' But the immediate danger was over.

Shada had appeared as if from nowhere and the zeal with which she protected her pal was total. A lifetime of placidity had disappeared in a moment as with teeth bared she stood firmly between David and his would be attacker.

When roused, Erchie Sutherland had shown that he found rational decision making difficult, but there was no way he would try to get past the angry mongrel.

Old Davy appeared, his trousers pulled over his nightclothes, a lantern in his hand. He looked every one of his sixty-four years as he surveyed the scene. The children, their fully clothed bodies apparent to all, skulked from the bed towards the old man. Shada kept his teeth firmly bared.

'It's time you sorted this grandson o' yours oot, Random,' he growled keeping one eye firmly on the dog. 'He canna jist come swannin' up here and hae his evil wye wi' whoever taks his funcy. And if he tries ...' His voice rose a decibel. Shada rebared her teeth.

David glanced at his grandfather. The look of disappointment on the old man's face when he first entered the room had been evident but had long since gone, now that he squared up to Erchie Sutherland.

'Dinna be ridiculous. Erchie. My grandson is twelve years old. And though I say it mysel' my dochter has made a grand job o' bringin' him up. A' by hersel'. The only time we ever hae ony trouble wi' him is fin he is wi' that quine o' yours.' Davy continued. 'Bit he seems ti be afa fond o' her so there's nae much we can dae. You should count yir blessin's when ye can, Erchie. Helen's nae gaun to be interested in the likes o' David for much langer, and then yir troubles will begin.

You'll achieve nithing by chargin' aboot like a bull at a gate, every time yir upset, Erchie. You've alarmed my wife the nicht, and damaged my door, and I'm telling yi' if you'd touched that loon, yi' wid have had P.C. Willie Grant tae deal wi' efter the dog and I had finished wi' yi.

Your Helen is a spirited lass, Erchie and she winna be easy for the next twa three years but why dae yi' nae listen ti one that kens. A quine like that needs a father she can spik tell, nae one that's at her throat every time she shows a bit o' mettle. Believe me, Erchie; you'll only get one chance.'

His long speech now delivered, David noticed a quiver of emotion developing on his grandfather's lip.

Erchie and Helen quietly made their way home, not exactly hand in hand, but at least David no longer felt worried about her safety.

Granda was not in an expansive mood. 'I think it's time that you were in yir bed,' he said to David. 'Ti sleep.' he added, as he turned away.

As David went to turn off his radio he learned that Cliff Richard had reached number one with "Living Doll".

16

Best Laid Schemes

Granny stretched the chicken wire firmly across the wooden frame that she had shown David how to make.

'Use the staples,' she encouraged him. 'And make sure you keep it tight.'

David had been assured that today was the day; twenty-eight days after the eggs had been entrusted to Alma's care. There would be ducklings by bedtime.

Under Granny's instructions he was making a small run in which the ducklings could enjoy the fresh air safe from predators of which there were several.

'Worst of a' are the craws. They could eat the lot in an hour given half a chance. Baby ducklings are a craw's favourite treat. That's why there are si mony o' them to start wi'. Some micht survive to keep the species going.' confided Granny.

David recalled how some four years ago, he and his Mum had travelled on the last ever tramcar from Portobello to Levenhall on the far side of Musselburgh, east of Edinburgh. They had taken a picnic for the long walk home: there being no tramcar!

They had fed bread to the ducklings that swam with their mothers by the mouth of the river Esk and David had been amazed at how many of them there had been. The ducks were mallards and a book David had at the time told him that they regularly produced clutches of eggs between eight and thirteen in number.

The ducklings, which were currently being born, were known as Khaki Campbells, a domesticated breed famed for the number of eggs that they laid and which to David's untrained eye, looked remarkably like the mallards of Musselburgh.

'Well done, loon!' smiled Granny as the final staple was hammered in place. 'We should have had this done weeks ago, I'm nae sure why I kept putting' it off. Noo let's get to that shed, I think there micht be a surprise waiting for you.'

And a surprise there was. Amongst the broken egg shells two ducklings had emerged, perfect specimens in obvious good health. Alma, her immediate work over, kept a motherly eye on the proceedings, clucking contentedly and apparently unconcerned that her offspring were the proud processors' of webbed feet!

'Why don't you go and drag a bale of straw in and mak' yirsel' a seat?' asked Granny. 'Ducklings are almost always born during the day. They'll a' be here by nicht.' She bent down and picked up one of the tiny down covered creatures in her hand. 'Isn't life wonderful?' she asked, almost to herself.

With Shada at his heels, David fetched the bale, and by the time he returned, Granny had gone back to the house. Fully engrossed in the birthing process, boy and dog settled down for a long wait.

At regular intervals throughout the next few hours, tapping noises would be heard, an egg would crack and as mother hen, dog and city kid looked on, a new life would force itself on the world. David was enthralled.

Gone, as if they had never existed, were the Princes Street throngs and maroon buses of his native city. Forgotten were the smells of the common stairwell, the greasy chip bags and fermenting barley with which he was so familiar. This was nature, doing pretty much as it had done, since the beginning of time.

David was mildly surprised that he had only one visitor to the shed that eventful day. His granda, strangely distracted, arrived, bringing him a whole bottle of lemonade and two crudely made cheese sandwiches. It was the first time in his life that David had seen him do anything so domesticated! Surprisingly, Granda did not appear to view the miracle of birth with the enthusiasm that David had imagined, and he shortly excused himself.

'Oh well,' David reasoned, 'from the beginning, "Project Duckling" had belonged to my granny and me.'

112

Eventually, it seemed to David that the miracle was over. Three eggs had shown no sign of hatching and were much cooler to touch. For whatever reason they did not contain live ducklings and David felt sure that his granny would probably remove them tomorrow. On the plus side, there were eight, lively ducklings, looking beautiful and already pecking at the seeds that had been provided for them. In their natural state, and with an aquatic mother, they would probably have been ready for their first swim.

The old zinc bath! It had stood outside, some twenty yards or so from the shed for many years, filled with rainwater and providing welcome drinks for Shada, Tibbie and any variety of animal life that cared to pass. Perhaps it could give the ducklings their first swim!

But David didn't know. He would have to ask his granny. For the first time he realised how much she had missed. She had seen only two ducklings, now there were eight. Whatever she had been doing for the last few hours, she was needed here now! With a cheerful good bye to Alma and her new brood, he whistled to Shada and skipped light-heartedly towards the house. It had been a good day.

****

Something was wrong! David felt it as soon as he saw the house. For the first time ever two cars stood outside the door. One was Nurse Burnett's now familiar Morris Minor, the other was larger and grander looking and completely unknown to David.

And could the old man emerging from the house be his beloved granda? David had seen him barely two hours before and although he had not been at his best he was still the granda that he had known all his life. Now he looked twenty years older. Slowly, purposefully and bent almost double he dragged himself towards his grandson.

David was afraid. What was the matter with Granda? Was that Mrs Johnstone he saw in the house? She had never

113

been to visit before. What was happening? Something was wrong!

'It's your grunny,' he said simply as he reached David. 'She's awa.' He averted his head quickly but not before David saw the tears flowing freely down his wrinkled old cheeks.

David did not understand. His grandmother was away. Where had she gone? And why the big drama? There was so much he needed to ask.

He said nothing.

Both David and his grandfather were relieved to see Sandy Stronach alighting from his bus, which had now taken up all of the remaining space outside the house.

'Well, Random,' he almost whispered, 'it's an afa', afa' business.' He shook Granda's hand and muttered something else, before turning to David.

'Now, Colonel,' he said quietly, 'I think you and I should go for a walk.' He held out his permanently gloved right hand, and David, forgetting he was twelve and a bit gladly held it.

It felt normal.

As they walked down the cart track and past the pothole in which Tibbie had recently so nearly lost her life, the kindly bus driver explained what he could to David.

His grandmother had died some three quarters of an hour ago despite the best attentions of Maggie Burnett and Clifford Brown, her family doctor who owned the other, grander car. She had died, a little earlier than expected, but after a long illness that had caused her a lot of pain. Her death had been peaceful and she had enjoyed telling Maggie about the ducklings only minutes before she slipped into unconsciousness.

Furthermore, Sandy's wife, Doreen had already managed to contact the hospital in Edinburgh where David's mother worked. She had been off duty, but the assistant matron who had taken the phone call promised that she personally would make the journey to Leith Walk and give her the sad news. Sandy was certain that Peggy would be back in

Balcrannie in a day or so as soon as she could make her travel arrangements.

Gradually, things started to make sense to David. He had accepted without question the fact that Maggie Burnett had somehow become a family friend even although until she had picked him up at the station just over a month ago she had practically been a stranger. Clearly she had been attending his grandmother on a professional basis with the fact that they got on well being a fortunate bonus.

As far as Granny herself was concerned, there had been ample clues that she was not in the best of health, but David had ignored or downplayed them all. Now he would never see her alive again.

David hesitated to ask the next question yet sensed that Sandy was the person most likely to give him a straight answer; provided, of course, he knew himself.

'Sandy,' David began hesitantly, 'what was it? What was it that killed my granny? Whit was wrang with her?'

Sandy shrugged his shoulders and looked genuinely sorry for his young pal.

'I dinna ken the answer to that, and if Doreen kens, then she's nae lettin' on,' replied Sandy thoughtfully. 'That's often the wye wi' women's health problems, David, maybe we're better nae ti ask ower mony questions. Your grandparents have been married for, what is it, more than forty years, but I bet there's things she' never telt him, health wise. A' I ken aboot my ain Mither's death is that she had "women's troubles". It's no' a lot ti go on, especially wi' me being on the ither side o' the world at the time. I've just got ti use my imagination, and who knows? I maybe imagine things that niver happened. Maybe yir mither will tell you more when she gets here the morn, bit dinna bank on it. Folk are particular aboot whit they tell one another aboot their ailments and that's maybe no' a bad thing.'

Something was bothering David and he could contain himself no longer.

'Sandy,' he spluttered, ' there was a bit o' a scene last night wi' Helen in my bedroom. Granda seemed terribly

115

disappointed in me. You don't think I killed her? Wi' a broken heart or something?'

Sandy had heard nothing about the "Top Twenty" incident and once again was reliant on his imagination. What could the pair have been up to now? They certainly seemed to have a knack of getting into trouble when they got together, so he supposed something like this was only going to be a matter of time.

'You city slickers,' he said with a smile he did not feel, 'whatever next? And I thocht she was savin' herself for Elvis Presley. He's gaun ti' be afa upset when he hears o' this!' He caught David's eye and could see he was desperate for reassurance. He held David's' head in both his hands and knelt down to his height.

'Listen carefully, Colonel,' he said slowly and precisely. 'I dinna ken whit you are spikin' aboot, but no, yi didna kill your granny and neither did yi' brek her hert. Abody in Balcrannie kens that you're the aipple o' her ee'. She deid afa' pleased that she kent you, and remember, as lang as you live there's a bit o' her gaun aboot. So you dae her prood, Colonel.'

Suddenly it struck Sandy that up until now, David had shed no tears for his grandmother, but now his eyes were brimming.

'It's a' richt, David, he said, for once giving him his correct name. 'You hae a good greet. I often do.'

David wept.

Hours later, as Sandy drove his bus home, he reflected on the "bedroom incident" with a smile.

'Twelve years of age,' he grinned. 'I wis still collectin' stamps!'

116

- 17 -

A Brave Face

For the first time ever, David could see that he had caused Helen some embarrassment. They were sitting by the "Pirate Ship" on the morning after the worst day of David's life.

'It wis, yi ken,' she spluttered, reddening and pointing to the general direction of her chest, 'her breast.' There she had said it!

David was momentarily taken aback but welcomed the opportunity to look legitimately at Helen's breasts, something he had been slyly trying to achieve for the last month. Undoubtedly Helen's acquisition of these appendages over the previous twelve months had been one cause of the awkwardness that occasionally sprung up between them this year. Now he could have an eyeful, albeit through her dress. It was not the kind of thing he should be enjoying, he chided himself, with his grandmother dead for less than a day.

'My mither says your granny had a growth in her breast,' she finished lamely.

David had never met Helen's mother and somewhat resented the fact that she had apparently been freely discussing his grandmother's ailments while he had been completely unaware of their existence.

'What else did she say?' he asked, desperate to have any details despite his disapproval of the gossip.

'She niver telt a soul, nae even yir Granda until it was far too late. I believe it was bleedin' and a' festered before she ever mentioned it. That's why Muggie Burnett was coming every day. Ti pit a dressin' on it. Oh David, come here,' she said, encircling him in her arms and pulling him tight. 'I thocht yi must 've kent.'

David was confused. At the very moment that he was discovering the pleasure of being held next to Helen's breasts he had to accept that his granny was lying dead, killed by the

117

self same part of her anatomy, bleeding and suppurating. David blamed God!

'I suppose you think you're really clever, you auld bastart!' he yelled skywards, as he broke free from Helen. 'You didna need to kill my granny. What did she ever dae to hurt you? She could have lived for another twenty years.' He looked rather embarrassed at his outburst. 'Oh Helen,' he said, collapsing for a second time into her arms. 'It wisnae God that killed her, it was me!'

David's relationship with God had deteriorated over the years. As a very young child he had been taught to say his prayers diligently. Every night he had asked for God's blessing on all his family members, even his mystery uncle Ted, somewhere in India. David hoped God would know how to get in touch with him even although no one else did, but he had very little to go on.

Then one night, David forgot to say his prayers. The next morning, the sky had not fallen down, there were no reports of earthquakes in America and perhaps more importantly from David's point of view, the telly had not blown up!

From then, it was much easier to "forget".

David stopped saying his prayers completely and made excuses to avoid accompanying his mother on the very rare occasions that she went to church. It seemed somehow irrelevant.

David cringed when he recalled the last time he had tried to evoke God's help. His beloved "Dons" as Aberdeen Football Club was usually called, had been due to play Glasgow Rangers in an important match and he had prayed for victory. He had even tried to broker a deal with God that he would go to church the next time he was asked by his mother if his prayers were answered. But Rangers won 3 – 0. David decided that God must be too busy to worry about such trivia, or more worryingly that he might have a soft spot for Rangers. He dismissed it as harmless fun, but perhaps it was pay back time.

The fact that it was a breast that killed Granny was, David decided, deeply significant. He had been much too interested in them recently. His curiosity over Helen was a good example, but there were others; actresses on television, people in the street and the assistant from Haddington in the library. He had allowed himself to become distracted, and God had wreaked his revenge.

Tony Togneri had told David how he had to go to confession when he had "impure thoughts," which apparently was quite often. David was unsure what impure thoughts were, but he thought that he maybe thought them.

'Oh, Helen,' he was sobbing vigorously. 'What have I done?' he asked.

A very different Erchie Sutherland disturbed them

'I'm really sorry aboot yir grunny, David,' he said almost tenderly. 'Its an afa' business. I've jist been spicking to your grandfather,' he continued, 'and he wants you ti go wi' him to the toon in the denner time bus. You should maybe go and get ready. Dinna worry about yir dukies. Helen and I will see to them.'

His ducklings, the sources of so much joy only a few hours ago! David had forgotten all about them.

'Thank you, Mr Sutherland,' he gave a somewhat watery smile, 'I must see my grandfather'.

As David disappeared, Erchie turned to his daughter. 'That's a right good loon yi've got there,' he said.

****

Granda was pacing the kitchen floor, dressed in his ill fitting best suit and sporting a tiny piece of newspaper on his cheek to stem the flow of blood from a snick with his razor. He looked half his former size and the last hint of colour had disappeared overnight from his still ample head of hair.

He looked up as David entered the room.

'I'm gaun ti see Maisy at the Royal,' he explained, 'and I wint ti dae't afore yir mither gets here. I'll need ti catch the one o'clock bus. Will you come wi' me loon?'

David nodded his agreement, while trying to figure out what was happening. He vaguely recalled that the Royal was a Mental Hospital similar to the one in which his mother worked

119

in Edinburgh. It was situated in the Foresterhill part of town adjacent to a large general hospital and the hospital for sick children. Of the three, it was the poor relation, talked about in whispers or not at all by a population still largely ignorant about mental illness.

His great aunt, for David realised with a start that that was what she was, Maisy, was perhaps typical of the several hundred patients who lived there. David had never met her and Granda who was her nearest surviving relative had never mentioned her before.

Only once had Granny spoken about her to David and her story was a sad one. The youngest of the family, she had still been a girl at the start of the first World War which claimed the lives of two of her three brothers and not much older when the Spanish 'flu killed a sister and her mother.

She had already been acting strangely when she went to Fife to be near her only surviving sister Gladys and had first been hospitalised there at the age of twenty.

For reasons and at a time unknown to the family, she had eventually been transferred back to the Royal Cornhill Hospital, Aberdeen, where she lived until this day.

Only once, when Peggy and Uncle Ted had been quite young, the authorities had arranged for her to spend a week's holiday at Mossyhillock. She had locked herself in a hen house within hours of arriving and had stayed there for two days until the same authorities came and removed her. The experiment was never repeated.

Now Granda was determined that he, accompanied by David, would personally tell her of the death of her sister in law.

****

They boarded Sandy's bus at the crossroads with no name and sat silently three or four rows back. The journey was very different from the one made in reverse by David, a month ago, at the beginning of his holiday.

David pondered on the forthcoming visit with some trepidation, while Old Davy politely accepted the commiserations of several other passengers who had somehow already heard of Granny's death.

They alighted at the terminus at Mealmarket Street and turned left towards West North Street.

'I dinna ken the number o' the bus,' said Granda, who was an infrequent visitor to Aberdeen, 'but we'll walk it in twenty minutes.' Cap on head, he strode forward purposefully.

David was a stranger to this part of town, and in different circumstances, might have enjoyed the expedition. From West North Street they joined Hutcheon Street and shortly after crossing George Street, a main thoroughfare from the north, they passed the city's slaughterhouse, a place that smelled of death and was the final destination of hundreds of cattle every day. From there, they entered Berryden, the sight of a large diary, and passed through a side entrance into the hospital grounds.

The building before them was stark and Victorian, while in comparison, the grounds were immaculately kept, at least in part by a number of patients who worked at a leisurely pace under the watchful eye of a gardener.

The reception area was dark and forbidding, but the woman behind the desk gave them the instructions they required. They were sent along a corridor that doubled as a lean to greenhouse and contained hundreds of potted plants, again carefully looked after by someone who might have been a patient.

Maisy was in one of several wards at the end of the corridor, each contained behind a bleak, substantial and decidedly locked door.

Old Davy rang the bell. After a few moments, a male voice called out, 'Lena, can you get that?'

There followed much rattling of keys before the door was thrown open by the ward cleaner.

'Maisy?' enquired the cleaner a little incredulously. 'I haven't seen you here before. I'll see if I kind find her for you.'

David and his grandfather found themselves standing in a large soulless room, or ward where numerous individuals of either sex sat on seats placed unimaginatively around the walls or paced aimlessly about the floor.

A man in a grubby white coat sat at a table apparently engrossed in the racing section of an equally grubby newspaper, whilst another, at the far end of the ward struggled to shave an elderly patient whose arms seemed to flail constantly. David experienced a feeling of unease.

This turned to distaste, when what could only be described as a grotesque old man suddenly got off his chair and started ambling towards them. In his hand he held an ugly looking mask, which covered at least half of his face including his drooling mouth. It seemed like a scene from some macabre Shakespearean play or a masque ball from hell.

It was only when the hideous figure tried to put his free hand round Granda's shoulder and appeared to say something that the man in the scruffy white coat leapt to action. Allowing the racing section to drop at his feet, he grabbed the old man by his shoulders and without a word to David or his grandfather, began to guide him back to his seat.

'Lena,' he shouted, once again, 'Dae yi' ken if Dr McAlpine's still aboot? He needs ti hear about this!

Dr, McAlpine pulled his beard thoughtfully, and gazed from his office window.

'Tell me again, Hughie.' he demanded, turning to the now breathless man in the grubby white coat. 'He actually got out of his chair, approached the visitor and tried to speak to him? Incredible. I have been a consultant psychiatrist in this place for nearly thirty years and he has been mute for all that time. No one has ever heard him try to communicate with a single person, fellow patient, or staff member. How unfortunate that he chose to speak gibberish.'

But Wullie Reid had not spoken gibberish. The first words he had uttered in forty years were 'Gushet Neuk'!

122

- 18 -

A' Right

Mrs Johnstone was in full flow. 'I ken he has a lot on his mind, Shaddie, whit wi' his mither arriving this afternoon, but he surely didna think I was gaun ti miss oot on seeing these dukes o' his, did he?'

Shada looked intelligent and wagged her tail. David leapt from his bed, where he had endured another practically sleepless night to realise that he had overslept. Mrs Johnstone was standing by his window.

'My goodness, he's awake,' she continued to the dog. 'Well we'll go into the henhouse and see what's happening. He can follow us once he's got his breeks on.'

'Sorry Mrs Johnstone, I fully intended to ask you to see my ducklings, but the way things have been,' his sentence tailed off, his eyes filling with tears.

'He must think I'm a richt hard hearted auld wifie, Shaddie, and maybe a nosey parker in a', but he disnae ken the wye we dae things up here.'

She turned to David and addressed him directly for the first time. 'You've made a grand job o'the dukes, loon, and I ken your granny wid be afa' prood o' you.' Her voice became more serious.

'I ken your hurtin' inside, loon,' she said, 'but your grandfather is hurtin' even mair. There's nae mony as thrawn as Auld Random, but you and I are going to have to sort him oot. At least until your mither gets here the nicht.'

David looked uncertain.

'I've got a pot o' soup right here wi' me and the pair o' you are goin' ti hae that for your denner, or you'll hae me to argue wi.' Then your gaun ti tell me where your granny keeps her spare bed linen and we're gaun ti mak a nice welcomin' bed up for your mither's arrival. It cannae have been easy for her being doon there on her own when she got the news. She'll be missin' you, David.'

She looked again at the dog. 'Whit dae you think he's waiting for Shaddie? Dae you think he's gaun deaf?' Shada wagged her tail in a non-committal looking way.

'Well are you going to help me or no?' she asked David.

To his surprise he heard himself reply. 'I'll help you on one condition. That you tell me what you know about the Burma Star Association. Sandy just dries up when I ask him about it.'

Mrs Johnstone shook her head gently. 'My you're a strange one,' she murmured. 'I'll dae my best, but I'm nae sure there's much I can tell yi'. Noo whaur did your granny keep her blankets?'

Mrs Johnstone was as good as her word. By early afternoon she had ensured that Granda and David had eaten several plates of her soup while she herself had worked wonders on the spare bedroom. Peggy would be impressed.

But more importantly, from David's point of view, she spoke; and then she spoke some more.

David was enthralled.

At the start of the Second World War, the authorities had made a decision not to create "friends battalions" that had proved so disastrous in the First World War. Then friends had been deliberately recruited and sent to fight together in a strategy planned to encourage them to enlist. This plan had spectacularly backfired when casualties were high, with families, streets and entire villages sometimes losing all their young men in the course of one bloody day's battle.

The names of these unfortunate young men could be seen on cenotaphs or war memorials in every town or village throughout the country.

Yet this change of policy had only been partly successful and friends did find themselves fighting side by side in the Second World War. For instance the quarry at Balcrannie was the largest single employer in the parish and its employees were encouraged to enlist early on with a promise that they would be used only for road building. In event they were captured near Dunkirk at the beginning of the war and most of them spent the entire conflict as prisoners of the Germans.

Many others, including her future son in law Sandy Stronach, Bertie Hamilton and perhaps even David's own uncle Ted had joined the Second Gordon Highlanders and in due course, found themselves defending the apparently impregnable fortress of Singapore.

Singapore was not impregnable and those who escaped death in the initial conflict found themselves prisoners of the Japanese.

These young men suffered unimaginable cruelty, forced labour on the construction of the Burma Railway, and starvation diets. Many did not survive life in the searing heat.

Of those who finally made it back to Great Britain, many were broken men. Some spoke at length of their experiences, but most, like Sandy Stronach, refused to say a word.

The medal issued to these young men to mark their experience was called, presumably because of its appearance, "The Burma Star" and Burma Star Associations sprung up throughout the country.

Mrs Johnstone knew little about what they actually did because Sandy never discussed it with her but she believed they had a welfare function for ex soldiers who were unable to work or who had fallen on hard times. It also, she believed, provided a forum for former comrades to meet together and keep in touch. As long as people kept the memory alive perhaps it would act as a stark reminder of man's capacity for inhumanity to man and might help prevent a repetition. It seemed to provide Sandy with a focus for his energy and memories.

Sandy's wholehearted support of the Association but reluctance to speak of his experiences seemed to be typical of many of the former POWs according to Mrs Johnstone.

'One more thing,' asked David delighted to have so much historical information, 'Why does Sandy always wear a glove on his right hand?'

The old woman's expression changed. 'You'll need to ask Sandy aboot that yoursel'.' she replied.

****

Old Davy *was* hurting. The trauma of the last day or so, borne, apart from his young grandson, largely alone, set him thinking. And as always in such key moments in his life, he took to the hills. Or rather the upper field that overlooked his small croft. In England he believed, they would have called it a knoll but here it was a brae or a hillock.

Shada, as sensitive as ever, had abandoned David with Mrs Johnstone to provide companionship to her master in his solitude.

He surveyed his croft from the top of the hillock. It had been his home for thirty-five years and sometimes he had hoped that he would still be living there in another twenty. Now with his dearest Elsie gone, he was not so sure.

The chance that had taken him to Balcrannie in the autumn of nineteen fifteen proved fortuitous. He had felt instantly at home in the nondescript parish with its old fashioned farming ways, its salmon fishing and busy stone quarry.

Peter Byers, his boss at the estate proved to be a demanding but fair employer with a shrewd talent for assessing the merits of those in his charge. He quickly realised that Davy, despite his serious accident, was everything an employee should be, honest, hard working and appreciative. The two men developed a firm friendship based on mutual respect.

Tragedy however was not confined to the fields of France and Peter was dealt a grievous blow when his wife died without warning towards the end of the following year. Heartbroken and undomesticated, his very existence might have been threatened had it not been for his niece, Elsie

126

Cunningham moving in as his housekeeper. It had only been a few months since she had heard of the death of her fiancé, Robbie Greenhowe and she harboured no expectations from life other than the opportunity to be of assistance to her uncle.

Out of respect for his fallen comrade, Davy had avoided getting close to Elsie for what seemed like forever, but their's was a match made in Heaven.

There was no question of Davy working anywhere else after the war was over, with the Laird, now carrying a serious injury, quickly coming to share Peter Byers' high opinion of him. He married Elsie in 1920 and set up home in what had been the groom's quarters, right next to the big house.

When Mossyhillock, the smallest holding on the estate, became vacant in 1924, the Laird had been keen that Davy and Elsie would apply for the tenancy. Safe in the knowledge that it would be farmed properly and looked after meticulously, he offered the young couple six months' free rent. They moved in shortly after along with baby Ted who was nearly six months old. Peggy was born nearly three years later.

Davy reflected on the hard but rewarding life they had led there and the unlikely chain of events that had led to him buying the croft some three years ago in 1956. He smiled, "Davy and Elsie Gordon, landowners," had an impressive ring to it, although even now, there was still a great deal of basic modernisation to be completed.

But now he had a funeral to oversee and countless personal tasks relating to Elsie to undertake. He wouldn't know where to start. Peggy would be arriving later tonight, now he would really know if the harsh words spoken some thirteen years ago had been forgiven

David had bought a platform ticket and was now eagerly scanning every passenger as they disembarked from the Edinburgh train. He was grateful beyond measure to Maggie Burnett for making the detour to Mossyhillock to pick him up before going to the Joint Station to meet Peggy. He was desperate to be with his mum.

127

Suddenly he saw her. She was lugging a heavy suitcase and wearing a coat that made her look every inch a nurse even although it was a leisure time garment. Her face seemed paler, and her shoulder length hair was rather severely tied back, but David was sure that he could still just about detect a hint of the customary twinkle in her eye.

Compared to Maggie Burnett's bear hug of a month ago, David's reunion with his mother seemed positively sedate.

'A'right, wee man?' asked Peggy, letting the suitcase drop at her side.

'A'right.' he nodded, snuggling close to her body.

- 19 -

Detente

Peggy discovered that there was a lot to do and not a lot of time to do it. A funeral had to be arranged, and she had no direct experience in such matters. Granda had done very little in the two days following Elsie's death, although the funeral had been tentatively arranged for Friday. Today was Wednesday.

Peggy had been up since the first bird had initiated the morning chorus, and David had found himself tufted out of bed shortly thereafter. He was of course, used to his mum's no-nonsense, "let's get on with it approach" and now welcomed it more than ever. He had missed his mum.

Despite her best efforts, Mrs Johnstone's bedroom arrangements would last for one night only. The undertaker had removed Granny, or at least her body, shortly after she had died and she was currently in a chapel of rest some twelve miles away.

Peggy wanted her back until the funeral. It was the custom in Balcrannie for the deceased person to remain at home, with the coffin open, until the day of the funeral and Granda was pleased that Peggy had organised that. He had simply said nothing and let the professionals take control, now the family was back in charge.

Granny would be kept in the spare room, where Peggy had spent the previous night. Her coffin would be displayed on a raised trestle and it was anticipated that many friends and neighbours would call in the next two days to pay their respects.

Peggy would sleep in David's bed in his lean to room and he would be relegated to the living room sofa.

'Unless, Helen Sutherland gives you a corner o' her bed.' Peggy remarked, her face deadly serious. Someone had been talking about the "Top Twenty" incident!

129

Just in time, David noticed a hint of a smile on his mother's face and he blushed, although he was not entirely sure why.

****

The first of many visitors to arrive that day was the Reverend Sylvander Crowe astride his BSA Bantam motorcycle which phutted unconvincingly wherever he went but was extremely economical on fuel. Whether in his motor cycling leathers or his working suit, the reverend was invariably dressed in black, a look that was exaggerated by his unfashionably long, raven coloured hair, which protruded from below his crash helmet. He was known, unimaginatively as "The Craw".

David slipped quietly out, on the arrival of "The Craw". H e could not endure the thought of praying for his granny or being subjected to any more "Top Twenty" innuendo. Shada and the "Pirate Ship" beckoned.

Peggy and Old Davy, however, although neither of them was normally religiously inclined, seemed to welcome "The Craw" and ushered him gratefully indoors. There was much to be discussed.

The announcement was due to appear the following day and the funeral service would take place at one fifteen on Friday afternoon, here at Mossyhillock.

Internment would follow in the local churchyard some two miles away, at two thirty.

All family, friends and neighbours were respectively invited.

"The Craw" muttered a prayer, shook hands and left. He would see them on Friday. Granda wandered aimlessly towards the corn yard. Peggy went looking for a bucket of hot water, a scrubbing brush and some soap. She had set herself the task of ensuring everything was spick and span.

If a visit from a motorcyclist was something of a rarity at Mossyhillock, two on the same day was unheard of. Yet,

130

just after lunch, a remarkably similar looking machine phutted to a halt just outside the door.

Granda's face visibly blanched. 'You get it, Lass,' he indicated to Peggy. 'Nothing good ever come oot o' a telegram.'

Peggy tore the telegram open, glanced at the contents and then somewhat exasperatedly mouthed the word 'Ted.'

Precisely, she read the message.

REGRET NEWS OF MUM + STOP + IN UGANDA+ STOP + IN SUGAR + STOP + CANT MAKE GB + STOP + RADHIKA WIFE RATNA AND NILIMA DAUGHTERS SEND LOVE + STOP + LOVE TO WEE DAVE + STOP + TED

Granda covered his face with his hands and sunk into his seat. 'He's married a native. I've two half castes for granddaughters.' he gasped brokenly.

Peggy was furious at her brother. 'Naebody's iver called him Wee Dave,' she fumed. 'He never thinks o' anybody but himself! I think these are Indian names, Dad,' she added. 'He must have got married in India right enough, but what they're doing in Africa, God alone knows!'

David was ecstatic! His "mystery" uncle had asked for him by name and he had two cousins somewhere in Africa.

For the first time ever, he didn't feel alone!

Just before teatime, another important visitor arrived and he wore a most worried expression on his face. It was Patrick Hay the undertaker and he was driving his old Standard Ten car.

'The hearse is aff the road, Davy. Blawn a gasket,' he said with a mournful expression entirely in keeping with his chosen profession. 'And the ane we usually hire in emergencies is spoken for a' day. To tell you the truth, Davy, we're struggling.'

Granda had not recovered from the earlier news from Ted and seemed at breaking point.

131

David piped up. 'Why don't we use Tibbie instead? Granny really loved that auld horse. Tibbie could do it.'

' Be quiet,' Peggy interrupted, 'we have a problem here. You and your daft ideas!'

But for the first time in that horrible week, Old Davy was smiling.

'Brilliant, Loon,' he said with what sounded almost like enthusiasm. He turned to Mr Hay. 'Jist mak' sure you and your assistant are here, Paddy. We winna need your hearse.'

David's brilliant idea had come at just the right time to jump-start Granda out of his inertia. Very early next morning he left on Fergie with the semblance of a smile on his face.

He returned mid morning positively grinning.

'I've been tae the Big Hoose,' he cackled, 'and it's still there!'

David would never have presumed otherwise, but quickly realised that it was not the Big House that Granda was referring to. In fact it was an ancient gun carriage that had seen service in the First World War and which the old laird had later purchased and forgotten about. It looked something like a table on two wheels with long shafts, which would hopefully fit Tibbie's substantial girth. It had stood forlorn looking with various dilapidated pieces of ancient farm machinery on what was little more than a rubbish dump for many years. It was in considerable need of a "sprucing up".

'It's being delivered this efterneen and we'll pit it in the neep shed. We'll need a pail o' soapy watter and plenty o' elbow grease, David lad, but we'll fair dae her prood.'

Peggy had been experiencing mixed feelings about the project and these were exacerbated when the old gun carriage finally arrived. She had had visions of her mother being taken to church in the box cart and would certainly put her foot down at that. The gun carriage would add a bit of grandeur to the proceedings but the funeral was less than twenty four hours away and it looked in need of a great deal of tender loving care.

132

But Peggy had a whole lot of other things on her mind. Any minute now her old neighbour and school friend Doreen Stronach and her more flighty sister, Marjory Johnstone, would join her. It would be great to see them again, despite the circumstances, and there was so much for them all to do.

The two men in her life could see to the gun carriage.

It was hard work. To be perfectly honest, David and his granda had achieved very little after almost two hours effort. The application of large amounts of soap and water, while getting rid of the surface dirt, seemed merely to highlight how far the once proud lady had fallen. Granda's newfound good humour was in danger of evaporating.

It was not improved by the entirely unexpected arrival of Bertie Hamilton carrying a sizeable cardboard box whose label indicated that it had once held tins of tomato soup.

'Fit dae you wint?' asked Granda with uncharacteristic abruptness. The two men appeared to be complete opposites. 'Are yi' agitating to start anither, General Strike or are yi' campaigning for tiaras for tattie howkers?' he continued with ill-disguised hostility.

David knew that the General Strike to which his Granda referred had taken place in 1926 and had lasted about a week, but nevertheless, it was seen as proof by the old man that organised labour and trade unions were a source of trouble. By implication, the Labour Party, that relied so heavily on Trade Union support and for whom Bertie worked were nothing but paid agitators who were bound to bring doom to the hard working common man. It was a point of view that would be barely understood in the industrial parts of the country but which, nevertheless was widely held in the North East.

Bertie was not rising to the bait. 'Come on Mr Gordon, your forgetting I'm half Donald. I think you could be doing with a hand.' he grinned. David was impressed.

Davy had in fact forgotten that Bertie was half Donald. His mother, the eccentric Mrs Hamilton, was the youngest child and only daughter of Alfie Donald, himself one of the well-known Donald dynasty of champion ploughmen. Bertie's uncles had continued the tradition and between them had won prizes at scores of ploughing matches throughout the land until gradually tractors had taken over and the interest in such competitions diminished.

This meant nothing to David, but the penny reluctantly dropped for his granda. Almost as important as the ploughing in these events were the appearance of the horses and equipment. Above the mantelpiece at Mossyhillock as in most farmsteads throughout the district was a large picture of a pair of Clydesdales, bedecked in ribbons, mane brushed and harness polished about to do battle at a ploughing match.

If Tibbie and the gun carriage were to be made presentable in time for Granny's final big day Bertie Hamilton and his Donald genes would have to be taken on board.

'I've got some black paint in the box here,' he offered, 'and if it dries in time, I could touch bits of it up with the gold stuff in this small can. I've got all the clippers, brushes, polish and stuff that we'll need for Tibbie and her harness, back at my mother's. That will have to wait until first thing tomorrow.'

Davy knew it was too good an offer to refuse and one that he scarcely deserved.

'Welcome, Comrade Trotsky,' he replied, with just the flicker of a smile.

The trio worked with gusto, with Bertie's knowledge and skill inspiring the others to greater effort. For the first time, it seemed possible that tomorrow's deadline could be met. Davy discovered that the young socialist's company was better than he could have imagined, and David silently plotted how he could get this real live politician to himself. He had so much he wanted to ask him.

Peggy appeared with the "fly cup" bang on cue. However busy she and her friends were indoors, this was one of Granny's traditions that she was not about to break. She was obviously surprised to discover that they had a visitor.

'Goodness, is that you, Bertie?' she squinted at the paint bespattered figure emerging from beneath the gun carriage. 'It's been a long time.'

'Peggy,' he replied, 'how are you?'

Some hours later, with the gun carriage looking remarkably impressive, Bertie again crawled from underneath it. He had been inspecting and lubricating the axle and wheel bearings that had stood almost idle for about forty years.

'I wonder, Mr Gordon, do you have such a thing as a torch? I just want to make sure.' He asked.

'David, rin into the hoose for a flashie,' said Granda preferring the more familiar Doric diminutive for a flashlight, 'yi' ken whaur it bides.'

David was only too happy to oblige his new found hero and raced to the porch where he knew the torch was usually stored. He was taken aback to hear a serious conversation coming from the kitchen. Despite the fact that Peggy had lost her mum and the funeral was the next day, the three women had been enjoying each other's company and David had thought, seemed almost light-hearted as they worked. Now the atmosphere appeared to have changed and David was sure that it was Doreen Stronach who was upset.

'Oh Peggy,' she was sobbing, 'I thocht he wid've grown oot o' it by noo, but if onything its worse. Nights are impossible, he demands that I keep the light on, and just when I think he's improving he'll have nightmares for several nights on end. He cannae bear ti think he is on his ain. I might jist be droppin aff and he starts shouting my name. He wakens the hale hoose.'

David had to return with the torch and any way was unsympathetic. Eck, the oldest Stronach child must be seven or eight, he was being quite unreasonable. Surely he could be giving his parents some peace by now?

It was just as well that he missed the end of the conversation. Doreen was now inconsolable.

'He'll seen be forty, Peggy. It's nivver gaun ti get ony better. They've robbed him o' the best years o' his life!

135

- 20 -

Earth to Earth

People started arriving very early on the morning of the funeral. Bertie Hamilton had applied the finishing touches to the gun carriage before eight a.m. and would be dedicating the rest of the morning to making Tibbie look as she had never looked before. He was taking the task very seriously indeed.

Doreen and Marjory had also reported for duty long before breakfast time with the additional promise that their mother Mrs Johnstone would be there before long to help with the considerable catering demands that were likely to arise.

Makeshift trestle tables had been erected in the barn, which was mercifully empty at this time of year, and an endless supply of broth, tea, cheese and sandwiches would be available all day.

David had been delegated to help Bertie and found pampering Tibbie to be very therapeutic. The old horse in turn, seemed to be delighted to have David for company throughout her unexpected transformation. David was, however, amazed at the amount of traffic that the funeral had engendered and kept a keen eye on all the comings and goings that morning.

Three times, unfamiliar vans arrived from one of the several larger villages that lay within a radius of some ten or twelve miles. They each delivered a number of wreaths and floral tributes from all manner of friends and relations. David had no idea that his granny was so well known or so popular.

He had also failed to realise the extent to which ordinary working people in Balcrannie were now becoming car owners, as a steady stream of mainly old cars arrived throughout the morning, bearing friends, commiserations and floral tributes. Many of the visitors were neighbours, but several came from considerably further afield.

Significant amongst those were the half brothers Gordon Baxter and Keir Wiley from the mining town of Kelty

136

in Fife. They were the sons of Davy's thrice married eldest sister Gladys who had died of cancer in Spain two years previously. David worked out that they must be his grandfather's nephews and therefore his mum's cousins, but he had never seen either of them before. They had hired a car and driven up, staying the night at Whitebraes, the only hotel in the parish of Balcrannie. They came bearing two bottles of whisky and a pair of large curtains made from Gordon tartan.

'You had better have these.' Gordon had said, handing the whisky to his cousin. 'I dare say you'll go through quite a lot of that before this day is over.'

Peggy was horrified. With neither her father or her being regular drinkers, it had never occurred to her to check the croft's whisky stocks, but it seemed likely that it would consist of what was left from Davy's annual "New Year" bottle of nearly eight months ago. It was the only occasion when alcohol was drunk at Mossyhillock.

It was one more thing for Peggy to worry about on this day that she wanted everything to be perfect.

The curtains were a thoughtful if somewhat bizarre present from old Mrs Rowan who owned Whitebraes. They had hung in the hotel for many years in an attempt to impart a sense of "Scottishness" to holidaymakers who may stay there. They had been discarded a few weeks earlier, and when Mrs Rowan heard from a customer about Tibbie and the gun carriage, she felt certain that, sensitively displayed, they could appropriately enhance Elsie's final earthly journey. After all, she had been a Gordon for nearly forty years.

From the other direction, Marjory Byers, wife of Elsie's late cousin Tommy arrived, unannounced from the beautiful but misnamed Black Isle. It is very green and not an island.

She was in her seventies and had driven down in a three-geared Ford Popular, which had seen better days. She was accompanied by her ancient West Highland Terrier, Lucy, but had otherwise made the journey alone.

Only strangers to Balcrannie would have been surprised to realise that, at the height of the morning's frantic

137

activities, Sandy Stronach had made one of his typical detours from his planned route.

For many years, local buses provided a vital lifeline between the city and outlying districts. Everything from newspapers to spare parts for cars were regularly despatched to country customers by bus and frequently left at road ends when the intended recipients were not on a bus route.

But Sandy's cargo that day was not going to be left at any road end. It consisted of at least eight further wreathes, including the family ones, ordered from a florist in King Street, Aberdeen and an important looking parcel addressed to Mr David Gordon, jun, Mossyhillock, Balcrannie. David had always considered himself to be Mr David Gordon (never mind the jun), Leith Walk, Edinburgh, but today, as he prepared to say goodbye to Granny, he was moved to have his Balcrannie origins confirmed in writing.

He wept.

The parcel, once the outer, brown paper wrapping was removed, revealed a large paper bag the outside of which proudly read "The Fifty Shilling Tailor". Inside, were David's first ever long trousered suit and a black tie. It was at that point that David suddenly realised that he had previously given no thought as to what he was going to wear at the funeral that was now less than two hours away. None of the clothes that he had been wearing all summer was even remotely suitable.

'I had to guess your size,' Peggy explained, all but overcome by the occasion. 'With a bit of luck your suit should do you until about this time next year. Your tie will last for life.'

The wreaths, now numbering close on thirty, were all absolutely beautiful, a result partially from the time of year which meant that there was almost an unlimited choice. The immediate family's tributes were even more special and David was astounded to see his own one, about which he had known nothing.

The word "Granny" was spelt out in exquisite white carnations, Elsie's favourite, against a heartbreakingly simple green background.

'You're one will be going right up front next to Granda's,' Peggy informed him. 'She was an afa' prood granny.'

Approximately half an hour before the service "The Craw" arrived along with Mr Hay, the undertaker and his assistant for the day, Jimmy Knox, a final year apprentice joiner whose grandfather had worked with horses for more than fifty years. They were all in Mr Hay's Standard Ten.

By this time, the family, their relatives and close friends had taken their places in the croft's living room or kitchen. Granny and all the flowers were in the spare bedroom just next door.

As others arrived, they tended to drift towards the barn for a cup of tea or to stand just outside the door and open window where they could hopefully see and hear the proceedings. On several occasions David glanced out at the gathering crowd with awe. Most of them were men, and he realised that he recognised many of the faces, although today they looked very different. "Scrubbed up," David thought perhaps best described those coming to pay their last respect to his beloved grandmother. All were in their Sunday best, some carried bibles, their faces were shining with the unusual experience of a midday wash, their voices were hushed, their heads bowed.

He had to look twice before he recognised the couple that were just arriving. The man looked older and very much like most of the other men, slightly uncomfortable in his suit, wishing perhaps that he could be somewhere else. The woman was dressed in a black dress and black stockings and wore an understated hat on her head. She looked pensive and sought the reassurance of the older man who seemed very protective of her. In other circumstances, David decided the young woman would be beautiful.

It was Helen and an apparently much more refined Erchie Sutherland. She must have been wearing a dress of her mother's.

"The Craw" had already said a prayer or made some sort of announcement, in an effort, no doubt to put everyone at their ease, but David had not been concentrating and was not really sure what had been said, but now, at ten past one, Mr Hay the undertaker addressed those in the house. Quietly, sensitively he announced that he was going to close the coffin lid and asked if anyone close to Elsie wished to have a last brief moment with her alone.

Old Davy sobbed audibly but indicated with his hand that he had already said his final goodbye. Peggy turned away, with the faintest hint of a wail and clutched Doreen Stronach for support. That was why Doreen was there, right next to the family.

Only David spoke. 'Please sir, I would like just one minute alone with my granny, if that's all right,' he announced.

The room went silent, all eyes focussed on David, his mother and grandfather. Would they try to stop him? Was it a good idea?

Nobody did try to stop him and he entered the room after repeating that it would only take a minute. He approached his grandmother, unsure of what to do. The Togneris, he assumed, would have crossed themselves. He didn't know what that was meant to achieve, but he suspected it would have allowed him to focus and may have been comforting. He simply stood by the side of the coffin, and sobbing blindly, touched her hand.

'Goodbye,' he mouthed, almost silently.

But that was not why he had entered the room.

Quickly, he went to the table at the head of the coffin where his "Granny" wreath lay, as promised, in pride of place. He read again, the attached card that simply said 'Loving you always, David.' He produced his brand new fountain pen from his inside pocket. It had been bought with a view to him starting at Broughton High School in a fortnight's time. Deliberately, he changed the full stop to a comma and added "Ratna and Nilima xxx."

Granny had not known of her grandaughters' existence and their names had never been mentioned since that fateful telegram, but David felt sure that his little cousins should be included.

"Nilima" was partly smudged by a large teardrop.

The service appeared to be a great success. "The Craw" had done his homework well even although Granny had not been a regular at his church. The word picture he painted of Granny was just right and David was gratified to hear his own name mentioned more than anyone else. It felt like a family history lesson and an affirmation of his place in the grand scheme of things.

If Granny's own first choice of hymn, "Shall We Gather By The River?" was a little unusual and caused a frantic search for the tune in the minds of the mourners, the second, "Abide With Me" was entirely traditional.

The coffin was passed through the open bedroom window to avoid any unseemly manoeuvring in the croft's narrow corridor and doorways. The undertaker, his assistant and the two Kelty brothers carried it on their shoulders to the waiting gun carriage, resplendent in its black and gold paint and draped in the Gordon tartan. Tibbie looked magnificent. It was a wonderful send off.

Jimmy Knox led Tibbie by the halter in a way that would have made his grandfather proud and David, with his Granda and Peggy on either side walked just behind the flower bedecked coffin.

Many friends and neighbours filed behind them seeing the long walk to the churchyard as a fitting way to pay their respects. Others, in their cars, would take a different route without in any way interfering with the procession. They would be waiting at the churchyard when the main mourners arrived.

As the moment of internment swiftly approached, Doreen suddenly reminded Granda that they had forgotten to nominate the eight cord bearers who would gently lower Granny into her grave. It was a job invariably done by men.

Most of them were obvious choices. Granda would have the cord at the head of the coffin; David would hold the one at the bottom. The Kelty brothers would each have cord as would, Frank Anderson, their immediate neighbour and Bill Gray the foreman at the home farm. Two more bearers were required. Granda spotted his political adversity Bert Hamilton who had been so helpful with the horse and gun carriage standing close by.

'Mr Hamilton,' he said, swallowing his pride, 'would you do the honours?' adding quickly in way of justification, 'Your mither and us have been neighbours for nearly forty years.'

The identity of the eighth bearer was solved immediately when, with a back firing noise, Sandy Stronach rolled up to the churchyard in his familiar bus. Once again his passengers had been taken on an unscheduled mystery detour but this time none of them seemed to complain. The Gordons had been known to most of them for many years.

The service at the graveside was short, the mourners sang "The Lord's My Shepherd" then David and his fellow cord bearers gently laid his granny to rest.

Meanwhile, a mile or so along the bus route, "Mrs Jenners" was incandescent with rage and mentally composing a letter of complaint to the bus company. Tosh Stronach's oil remedy had not worked, and her back was playing up again. She was missing her doctor's appointment!

Viva Espagne

On the days following the funeral Peggy had a lot on her mind. She had taken a full week's annual leave, which meant that she would return to Edinburgh with David the following weekend.

In the meantime, she had to finish the clean up of the croft house and somehow put arrangements in place for her father who had forgotten any domestic skills that he may have had before marriage but who appeared to have little insight into the difficulties that may creep up on him now that he was on his own.

But at only sixty-four Granda would not appreciate the thought of anyone making arrangements on his behalf. It would require a diplomatic touch.

And then there was the dance. David it appeared had been looking forward all summer to the dance, organised by the Burma Star Association that was to be held next Friday. He seemed determined that she should come too, and Doreen Stronach, sensing a rare night out had also been pressurising her to attend.

'It will just be like gaun back fifteen years,' she had enthused, 'when we were a' young and daft'.

Peggy did not think that she would like to go dancing in some country backwater just one week after her mother's funeral, but it was a battle she sensed that she was doomed to lose. She would wait and see.

It was the Monday evening and Davy had spent a busy day in the cornfield with his scythe. The sun had shone and he worked long, "reddin' the roads," or clearing a track for the binder that would start harvesting his oats, any day now. The weather seemed promising and it looked like an early hairst.
He had not spoken about Elsie to Peggy, but as soon as he had finished his evening meal he had gone to the big press or

cupboard and began searching frantically amongst the many old books he had haphazardly stored there. He emerged triumphantly with a battered copy of "A Rose for Winter" by Laurie Lee that Elsie had found in the Church sale of work two years previously. It tells the story of the author returning to Spain fifteen years after he had fought there in the Civil War.

He was now pouring over it in the semidarkness while he nursed a glass of the Kelty brothers' whisky, well diluted.

'I'm thinkin' o' gaun abroad,' he remarked with exaggerated casualness, as Peggy brought him a cup of tea.

She recoiled in disbelief.

'You can't go abroad without leaving Aberdeenshire,' she retaliated. 'And you know how hard you find that. Don't you remember how homesick you were those six hours you spent in Edinburgh after David was born? Six weeks after David was born.' She added coldly. 'Anyway, what put that daft idea into your head?'

But Davy was not so sure that it was a daft idea although he would never have considered it if Elsie had still been alive. Whatever the wisdom of it, the idea had been put to him by one of his nephews from Kelty. Their mother's third husband, Joe Waites had come from Rochdale but had lived in Spain since the end of the war. He had a cottage that he made freely available to family members and his liberal definition of family meant that Davy would definitely be included.

'He's coming over here for a fortnight in October,' Keir, the younger brother, had remarked. 'Why don't you come down to Kelty for a week or two before that and you could go back out there with him?'

The idea appealed. But not to Peggy.

She had always secretly resented her father's reluctance to make the comparatively short journey to Edinburgh to visit her, and his distinct lack of enthusiasm at David's birth. Peggy often wondered what David would think if he knew that his granda and hero had not always been so enamoured with him, but that was a secret she would never share.

'Anyway, you would need a passport,' she retorted in a tone calculated to dampen his enthusiasm

144

David and Helen sat on the hen house floor, leaning against the bail of straw that had been his seat during the birthing process. The events of the past ten days meant that the ducklings had been rather more neglected than might otherwise have been the case. Not materially, of course, they were fed, watered and given all the fresh air they could crave for, but human contact had been strictly limited.

'I dinna believe it,' Helen gasped, and in fact she couldn't make up her mind whether she did believe him or not. 'You walked up to the auld wifie's door and knocked on it? And she answered it? Fit wye did yi' nae tak' me wi' yi'?

It had been as easy as that. After discussing, plotting and fabricating a complete fantasy, surrounding Mrs Hamilton for more than half his life, David had found a way of getting to meet her. He knocked at her door and she answered!

He was glad that Helen did not pursue his reason for going alone, the fact being that he had never thought of asking her along. He had not actually gone with the intention of speaking to Mrs Hamilton, but rather to seek advice from her son.

Ever since setting eyes on Bertie Hamilton at the illicit hare chase, David had been intrigued by him and even although or perhaps partly because, he had most likely discharged his shotgun in their general directions a few days later, his fascination remained. It was not common, in David's experience, to know a man, who knew people that held positions of power within a major political party. It seemed likely that he knew members of parliament, and if David understood the role of election agent properly, he had probably helped get them there.

To find such a man in Balcrannie, of all places, seemed too good an opportunity to miss.

David wanted to ask Bertie Hamilton about the possibility of becoming a member of parliament some time in the future. After all the new member of parliament for East Aberdeenshire whose boundary was less than three miles from Mossyhillock, Patrick Wolridge-Gordon was only twenty-one,

145

a mere nine years older than he was. Harold Macmillan, the disconcertingly popular Prime Minister, although a toff was also apparently of crofting origin despite the fact that his family now owned a massive publishing firm and he had gone to a top private school. But presumably he had never lived in a tenement block in a one-parent family. There was so much that David needed to know.

It had taken a long time for the door to be answered, and when it was, there was no sign of Bertie Hamilton. His mother looked disappointingly normal if perhaps slightly uncertain. She had no warts on her nose and her dress gave no hint of extreme poverty or great opulence. From what he could see of the house beyond her, it seemed, apart from a faint whiff of cats, nondescript.

She peered at him through her battered spectacles, removed them, and peered at him some more. When she spoke to him, it was not in any witch like incantation, but in English, or what passed for English in Balcrannie.

'He's nae here,' she said simply, 'and I canna mine faur he's gaun.'

Just as David had decided that that was the end of the conversation, she spoke again.

'Jist bide there a minute,' she instructed, 'I think I've got this bit o' paper, somewye.'

As, with considerable difficulty, she turned her aged frame and dragged herself back in the direction of her living room, David felt intensely guilty. Clearly, he didn't deserve to become an M.P. Neither Harold MacMillan nor Patrick Wolridge-Gordon, he was sure, would ever have pilloried or caricatured a helpless old woman for their own entertainment. And they were both Tories.

Eventually, Mrs Hamilton reappeared; waving a piece of paper that had been torn from an exercise book. She seemed uncertain of its contents.

'Ha'e a look at this. I've got my wrang glesses on,' she explained, handing it to David.

It was Mr Hamilton's itinerary for the week. It contained the message 'Mon' 'Abd' and 'Kings X' with times,

146

some eleven hour apart written next to them. Below, he had written 'Thurs'and similar details of his return journey. There was also the address of a London boarding house with a telephone number, although David had no idea how Mrs Hamilton would be able to access or operate a telephone should the need arise. At the bottom of the page he had scribbled 'Fri – dance.' It was no surprise that a confused old lady would have difficulty deciphering this scrawl.

To David, this scrap of paper opened a window to a whole new world. To the best of his knowledge he had never met anyone who had been to London and he imagined that if he ever went there it would involve months of planning and saving up. Now he knew a man who thought nothing of popping down to London for a business meeting and getting back in time for a Friday night dance! The world was shrinking fast.

David remembered his manners. 'Thank you very much. Mrs Hamilton. This is most useful. My name is David Gordon,' he continued, 'I have been living with my grandparents at Mossyhillock, ...'

Mrs Hamilton interrupted. 'Oh I ken fine fa' you are.' she said, adjusting her spectacles.

David couldn't help but see Helen in a different light since her grown up appearance at Granny's funeral. Now she looked a bit disappointed.

'What a lot o' nonsense we've spoken, a' these years,' she mused, 'and her just an eccentric auld wifie a' this time.' But she soon brightened up. 'You'll be tellin' me next that Sandy Stronach jist wears that glove because he's got cauld hands!'

David laughed. Sandy's right hand, permanently hidden in a black leather glove had also been the subject of much childish musing and wild speculation. Perhaps, they had decided, it actually concealed a hook, like the one featured in "Peter Pan", but on reflection, that seemed unlikely. It seemed unnecessarily complicated to drive a bus with a hook covered by a five-fingered leather glove, so there must be another explanation. Helen had always liked the theory that his right hand had been chopped off in an Arab country for stealing bread to feed his starving children. But as far as David knew, his children had lived all their lives in the Bridge of Don which was entirely Arab free and with Mrs Johnstone for a grandmother, they were never going to starve.

Mrs Johnstone's words came back to him now. 'You'll need to ask Sandy aboot that yourself,' she had said when David asked her about the permanently gloved right hand. That he decided was what he was going to do. It would be that simple.

****

Bertie Hamilton had not meant to intrude. It was Friday morning, the day of the dance, and he had called to see David. Somewhat surprisingly, his mother had told him about David's visit although it had taken her sometime to recognise him, her own son. But David was nowhere to be seen.

Peggy however was sitting with her head in her hands, leaning over the kitchen table sobbing unrestrainedly.

It crossed Bertie's mind that he might be able to slip away unnoticed, but the level of Peggy's distress alarmed him.

'Your mother?' he asked gently, as he pulled in the chair next to her.

Peggy looked startled but desperately tried to compose herself. Now that he was here and had seen her crying, she did not seem to mind Bertie's intrusion.

'I wish it wis my mother; I can just about manage that. It's that crazy father o' mine. He's gone to the post office in that tractor o' his, to get himself a form for a passport. He's never dreamt o' getting a passport before.' Her tears were flowing freely again.

Bertie nodded at the kettle on the fire. 'I see it's bilin',' he observed. 'Where do you keep the tea caddy?'

Tea made, Peggy found Bertie easy to talk to. Her father had received a letter from Kelty this morning and had not been at rest since. Joe Waites had a friend, a retired vet, who had started a donkey sanctuary in Spain. The local people

148

were not very sympathetic since many of them were very accustomed to seeing donkeys being harshly overburdened by their owners. The donkey sanctuary implied criticism of their traditional way of life and even those who were fond of the animals felt the need to stick together and resist the temptation to work for the old vet.

The offer was simple. After his harvest at Mossyhillock, Davy was invited out to Spain on an expenses paid holiday. If he liked the place and the people, there would be a job available helping to look after the donkeys over winter. There was little to offer in the way of wages but there was food and sanitary accommodation and a climate infinitely more hospitable than Balcrannie in winter. It was like 1915 all over again.

'He's completely lost his reason,' Peggy sighed. 'At this rate he will end up in the Royal wi' Auntie Maisy.'

Bertie's response was not what she had wanted, he seemed faintly smitten. 'Hold on, this might just work. Let's look at it from all angles.'

With his mother being in the vulnerable state that she was, Bertie had given much thought to the plight of old people living alone in substandard conditions.

Old Davy owned Mossyhillock, but by modern day standards it was barely habitable. If he were to continue to live there he would need to advertise for a housekeeper, but no woman could be asked to live in Mossyhillock in its current state. At a very minimum, Davy would need to find money to install electricity when it became available next year, to put running water into the house and crucially, to build an inside bathroom and kitchen. Demands for a cooker, washing machine and television would be likely to follow very quickly.

It was unlikely that Davy would have anything like enough money to finance those essential improvements, and the days of small crofts like his being able to provide a comfortable living were fast disappearing.

'Whatever, he does,' concluded Bertie, 'He's going to have a lot of hard decisions to make, and staying here is going to be hard. I take it you can't offer him a bed in Edinburgh?'

'You take it right. He says it's too far away for him. Spain on the other hand ...' She shrugged her shoulders in mock despair, but her natural good humour was returning. 'On the other hand you could always give up politics and sign up as his orra loon.'

There were, of course many reasons why Bertie Hamilton could not become Davy's "orra loon" or general farm servant, but Peggy's attempt at humour provided him with the opportunity to explain his trip to London. His mother had not understood.

'I doubt that won't be possible,' he said, faking sadness. 'Duty calls, I'm afraid. I will be leaving Balcrannie on Sunday.'

Bertie's meeting with important members of the Labour Party's top brass had resulted in an immediate change of plans. Everyone in the know was certain that a general election was imminent and from Labour's point of view, Macmillan, as the sitting prime minister, was disturbingly popular. He would also have the final say as to when the election would fall and would no doubt choose a date that would best enhance his chance of re-election.

Bertie was now a proven asset as an election agent and Labour had decided to target the seats that they were most likely to win. West Aberdeenshire would never be in that category so he would be moving on immediately.

'Three constituencies in the central belt, have been mentioned as possibilities,' he explained, 'I'm just about to walk down to the phone box at Balcrannie, to help them come to a final decision.'

Peggy smiled peekily, 'Thanks; you're a great listener. I take it I'll see you at the dance.'

- 22 -

Let's Dance

Even if the Victoria hall had been built in the final year of the reign of the monarch after whom it had been named it would still be nearly sixty years old. And it looked it. A functional, rather than beautiful building, it nevertheless hosted practically all the social events in the scattered parish of Balcrannie, although it was situated, inexplicably, some distance from all but a handful of houses.

From time to time over the years it had proved a popular venue for dances although the absence of a nearby pub and the fact that it was not on the bus route meant that it was currently slipping from favour.

Tonight, however it was expected to be busy. Sandy Stronach was one of several, popular local men who had given active service in the Far East, and Burma Star Association events tended to be well patronised.

Wattie Law must have been as old as the hall itself and had played at every imaginable type of social function in Balcrannie for as long as anyone could remember. His skill on the piano accordion was considerable although the casual observer could easily overlook this. Unlike the up and coming musicians of the next generation, Wattie gave absolutely no attention to his presentation or image. For years he had sat in the centre of the stage on a battered and unglamorous chair with a completely detached look on his face.

He went nowhere without his music stand which was erected right in front of him and which only ever held one tiny sheet of paper that if any smaller would surely have been called a scrap. Wattie's repertoire was extensive and nobody ever knew what was on the precious piece of paper.

His hair was disappearing fast and what was left of it was brushed forward in a doomed attempt to make it seem

151

more plentiful. He surveyed his world through a thick pair of NHS spectacles.

Wattie may have suffered from a medical condition or else simply extreme tiredness that never ceased to amuse his audience. Often with the floor packed and a dance in full swing, he would appear to fall asleep. The music would slow down and the dancers would struggle to keep time. Wattie would wake with a start, realise what was happening and thump out the next few notes at increased tempo in an effort to catch up. The dancers would again rush to respond.

Wattie's performances were distinctive.

But the times were changing, even for Wattie. Recently he had acquired an unreliable microphone and tonight a blind percussionist with half a drum kit accompanied him for the first time.

A home made notice scribbled on card and sat next to the music stand announced to the world: "The Wattie Law Combo".

Helen had looked forward to the dance more than anyone else and was she hoped, dressed in the height of fashion. She walked to the hall with David, chattering incessantly, but had warned him that she may not be able to spend much time with him at the event. She would, she explained, be meeting "the girls".

David understood but doubted if it was really "the girls" that she hoped to meet.

Two buses had been privately hired to take dancers from the city of Aberdeen and a variety of outlying districts. For once, Sandy Stronach was a passenger, sitting three rows back with Doreen, his wife, who was also in high spirits.

By nine thirty, the hall was filling up nicely with local people and a smattering of strangers. Women and young people made up the majority of those present but an influx of men was expected when the pubs shut at ten.

Of those already there, many of the men had half bottles of whisky protruding from their jacket pockets and they would sometimes stop to share mouthfuls with their friends as they danced or walked round the floor. Two stewards, or "chucker oots" guarded the doors but no one was refused admission. Those carrying alcohol would offer the stewards a slug from their bottles and entry was guaranteed.

As the evening wore on the stewards wore an increasingly contented expression on their faces.

Wattie Law and his visually challenged "combo" were in top form. Peggy was up every dance, sometimes with Doreen or Marjory, sometimes with any one of a number of men who wished to be her partner. Helen and "the girls" were in a corner, giggling, dancing amongst themselves, and exchanging banter with a number of slightly older boys standing a short distance away. She thought she recognised one of them as "Malky" from the wake of a few years ago.

David was alone but in good spirits. He went to buy himself a soft drink and was approached by a cross-eyed stranger who seemed to be a few years older.

'This place is amazing,' said the ugly looking youth, peering down his crooked nose at David and speaking in a pronounced but completely unfamiliar accent. 'How do these old guys earn a living in a place like this? he asked David, indicating to the dancers.

David thought for a moment, 'Farm servants, fishermen,' he explained and then he remembered Balcrannie's main industry, 'and oh, the quarry; half of these people are probably quarrymen.'

The stranger seemed impressed. 'Quarrymen?' he mused almost to himself. 'I must remember that.'

Just then he was summoned by a woman who spoke in exactly the same accent. David assumed it was his mother. 'Come on, John,' she ordered the cross-eyed youth, 'it's time we were getting back to the boarding house. We don't want to be driving on these narrow roads after dark.'

John was not happy. 'But Aunt Mimi,' he implored, pointing to Wattie Law. 'This guy is fantastic.' But it was to no avail, his aunt was pointing to the exit.

'I'm going to form my own band when I get back to Liverpool,' he muttered sulkily to himself, and pushing his hair forward in the style of his newfound hero, he slouched out of the building.

David had not noticed Helen dancing with a tipsy youth she thought looked like the pop star Billy Fury but who was fatter and had red hair. And he didn't see them going outside.

A natural lull had occurred in the dancing. Sandy Stronach, beaming bon homie, scrambled on to the stage. He was about to draw the raffle, but first had an announcement to make. Because of the generosity of those who had bought raffles and everybody present a sum of almost £59 had been raised for the Burma Star Association.

'And I can tell you,' Sandy paused unintentionally as he momentarily saw his colleagues in his mind's eye, 'it will be put to good use. But now as they say, for something completely different. I'm goin' to sing ...' a few groans could be heard from the floor. 'something that my good pal, the colonel here tells me is top o' the top twinty. And he should ken.' To David's embarrassment a few of those in the know tittered, while Sandy, at the third attempt managed to dislodge the mike from its stand and clutching it in his permanently gloved right hand, he warbled into song:

Got myself a cryin', talkin',
sleeping walkin', livin' doll,
She's got the rovin' eye,
and that is why,
she satisfies my soul.

He aimed an exaggerated wink in the direction of Doreen who gave out a girlish shriek and started jiving with her sister. The crowd roared. Doreen was ecstatic.

Wattie Law, leapt awake, cocked his ears for two notes, and struck up the accompaniment!

Take a look at her hair. It's real.
If you don't believe what I say, just feel.
I'm gone lock her up in a trunk,
So no big hunk can steal her away from me,
I've got the one and only walking talking,

The crowd roared again. It was time to draw the raffle.

The dancing had recommenced, couples were beginning to snuggle a little closer and Wattie Law was doing his own version of Bobby Darin's "Dream Lover".

Suddenly, a loud bang was heard coming from outside and everything was thrown into confusion.

Women screamed and held onto their partners. Men exchanged glances and several ran towards the door.

Within seconds, Helen burst into the hall, dirty, distraught and sobbing disconsolately. She looked frantically for David and threw herself into his arms. 'Oh David,' she sobbed. 'Get me oot o' here.'

Helen had been completely besotted with the tipsy youth after only one dance and imagined that she might be in love although minimal conversation had taken place between them. He introduced himself as Gary, a name unheard of in Balcrannie.

When he asked if she would like a drive in his "motor", she could think of nothing she would like better and in the euphoria ignored the alcohol on his breath and the fact that his "motor" turned out to be an ancient van. His kiss in the car park promised joy unimaginable.

Gary started the car and immediately grabbed Helen with one hand, roaring out of the car park in low gear. Helen was beginning to feel afraid. He braked sharply as they reached the entrance to a field that also acted as a passing place, stopped the car and set about trying to kiss her savagely. This was not what Helen had expected, nor was it what she wanted, she tried to struggle free.

Gary showed no sign of calming down, so she tore her nails down his face. He gave a wild scream, restarted the car and roared back towards the hall. He was so busy looking at her as he cursed, that he failed to negotiate the car park entrance and smashed hard into the concrete gatepost. That was the noise that was heard in the hall.

155

Incredibly, rather than get them both out of the car he set about trying to kiss her again.

'If it hadn't been for Mr Hamilton and your mother I don't know what would have happened she sobbed. Bertie and Peggy were by this time standing right next to them, Bertie bleeding slightly from his right knuckles. David couldn't understand. His mother? Mr Hamilton? He caught Peggy's eye.

'We had just gone for a walk,' she explained lamely.

'I think we had all better go home, ' suggested Peggy. 'You had better come in past Mossyhillock, Helen, and we'll get you spruced up. You don't want to be going home looking like that.'

'Oh, thanks.' Helen replied. She was a little girl again.

It was taken for granted that Bertie Hamilton would be accompanying them on the mile and a half or so journey to Mossyhillock. Initially Helen had walked with David, trailing just behind the adults, but the conversation was painfully stilted. At some point the order changed and as David walked ahead with Bertie, trying to bend his ears about careers in politics, the womenfolk lagged behind.

Helen slipped her arm through Peggy's and looked up at her face. 'Oh, Peggy she said, 'There's so much that I ken naethin' aboot. Whaur dae I go fae here?

Peggy gently patted the young girl's hand. 'Tell me a' aboot it,' she whispered.

They slackened their pace and soon David and Bertie were out of earshot.

When Peggy and Helen eventually made it back, Helen seemed much brighter and ready for the cup of tea that David had prepared for them. David seemed beside himself with excitement and determined to spread the news.

'Mum, Mr Hamilton is coming to stay in Edinburgh!'

Peggy looked expectantly at Bertie, 'Is this true? Is that what you wanted to tell me just before the crash?'

Bertie raised both hands in front of him in mock surrender. 'Guilty as charged,' he agreed. 'When I phoned H.Q. this afternoon they told me three constituencies were looking for an experienced election agent. Greenock, the Gorbals and somewhere in Edinburgh. I chose Edinburgh.'

'Why Edinburgh? The other two sound like safe seats to me.'

She thought she detected a fleeting blush on Bertie's face, but it may have been the paraffin lamp.

'Because there's going to be a lot of leaflets to be pushed through an awful lot o' doors,' he explained, 'and I was kind of hoping you two might lend a hand.'

'For the Labour Party?' she asked teasingly, but she could see the barely concealed excitement on David's face. 'I think we might manage that, but,' she nodded in the direction of the bedroom where her father was sleeping, 'just dinna tell General Franco there!'

They all laughed

- 23 -

Back to the Future

'Tell me, you'll always come back to Mossyhillock.' Helen pleaded. 'I couldna bear ti think I might never see you again.'

It was Sunday morning and Helen and David were sitting by the "Pirate Ship", that old fir tree where they had reacquainted themselves on the first night of what had proved to be an eventful summer. It was now two days since the trauma of the Burma Star Association dance and Helen had come to seriously doubt if she would ever again feel as comfortable in the company of a male as she did with this serious young schoolboy who was her best friend. His mother had proved fantastic too when it was most needed. She would miss them so much.

'I'll be back, don't fear, ' promised David. 'This place is in my blood, and besides,' he hesitated. 'I couldn't bear not to see you again either. I'll always come back.'

Helen slipped from the large branch of the tree on which they had both been sitting and planted a kiss on his forehead. 'Cheerio,' she whispered. 'Dinna try and follow me, I'm going home.'

She moved swiftly along the track, her shoulders heaving as she sobbed. Shada looked quizzically at her master. 'Let her go Shada,' he said huskily, turning his head so that the dog would not see his tears.

Helen stopped once. 'Goodbye,' she called blowing a kiss and disappearing.

David would always come back to Mossyhillock. If there was a Mossyhillock to which he could come back. But that was no longer certain.

How David wished that Granda's crazy flirtation with Spain was some sort of mental aberration, brought on by grief

158

and liable to disappear as quickly as it had come. But he did not believe that that was the case.

Granda had been busy since he received the letter from Spain and his arrangements seemed logical and sane. During and after the harvest he would sell off most of his farm animals. Frank Anderson had long wanted an extra field to make his own smallish farm more economical and would gladly buy or rent the croft. In the meantime he had promised to give Tibbie a home for as long as it was required. Mrs Johnstone had quickly stepped in to claim the ducklings. 'It'll be a proper homecoming for them,' she told Shada. 'Them have started off here as eggs.'

And that had left Shada. 'You'll be wantin' to come here and a' are yi, Shaddie?' she asked the dog. 'Jist ti keep an eye on the dukes, like.' Shada looked at her intelligently, but made no response.

'I'll tak' that as an aye then!' And that was that.

Maggie Burnett had yet again volunteered to take Peggy and David to the station, and they would be leaving at one o'clock to catch the two o'clock train. As it transpired, Bertie Hamilton would also be on that train, but he would be making his own way to the station. All that was left was lunch and some special farewells.

****

It had been hard to say goodbye to the animals and to his own little room that he may never sleep in again, but this was worse. Much worse.

Peggy's farewell to her father had been low key but friendly enough and now she sat next to Maggie Burnett, the engine already idling.

David and his granda faced each other solemnly and it was the old man who made the first move. In a way that was so unlike him, he crushed David firmly to his chest and held him there. Two sets of tears flowed freely.

'Tak' care o' yir mither, David,' he sobbed. 'She's much mair chicken-herted than she let's on. An' niver treat

159

her like that loon o' oors treated us. Mine that whitever else happens in this life, she'll always be yir mither,' He paused, then with great effort, said solemnly, 'I think you should ken, you're the best thing that ever happened ti yir grunny and me.' It was the nearest thing to a declaration of undying love that Davy would ever be able to make.

Afterwards, David would think of how much he would have liked to say in reply, but all he could manage was 'Cheerio,' as he hurried into Maggie Burnett's car.

Maggie's driving had improved immensely over the summer and the trip to the station was uneventful. Bertie Hamilton was already there, and had arranged a seat next to them. David didn't mind.

As the station clock edged towards two o'clock, one final surprise awaited David. As he peered from the open window of his compartment, he spotted Sandy and Doreen Stronach with their youngest child, Dottie, hurrying along the platform. They had come to say their farewells.

There was much handshaking and kissing between the adults and David had to take special care to avoid being kissed by Doreen while at the same time trying not to hurt her feelings. But time was moving on.

With some difficulty, Sandy stretched through the open window and placed both hands on David's' shoulders. 'Well Colonel, it looks like it's time for a strategic retreat.' His lips quivered imperceptibly as he ruffled David's hair. 'Simmer jist
widna be the same withoot yi.'

But the whistle had already been blown and the train was now in motion. Peggy and Doreen yelled their farewells and made noisy arrangements to keep in touch. David waved only once, as the train negotiated the first corner and the platform disappeared from sight.

It was then that he remembered. He had forgotten to ask Sandy Stronach why his right hand was permanently gloved!

Historical Footnote

A General Election *did* take place that year, on October 8th, and resulted in a landslide victory for Harold Macmillan's Conservatives.

James Hutchison Hoy (Labour) and Patrick Wolridge-Gordon (Conservative) were re-elected to Edinburgh Leith and East Aberdeenshire respectively. 'Balcrannie's' West Aberdeenshire elected a new Member of Parliament, Alexander Forbes Hendry (Conservative).

Nowadays, he is perhaps best remembered for the bowling trophy that bears his name and which is competed for annually amongst the bowling clubs in his former constituency.

David Gordon travels from his native Edinburgh to his grandparents' Aberdeenshire croft for his summer holidays. It's something he has done for years. but now that he's twelve – he's making the journey on his own. It's 1959 and as this evocative tale unfurls the reader is tempted with a hint of romance and

brought face to face with tragedy. It's a summer of renewed acquaintances, a special birth and a mysterious encounter with a stranger It tells of a time when people were closer to the land with electricity and television becoming commonplace – but not for everyone.

An Early Hairst

Vividly and amusingly recalls a lifestyle that is still fresh in the minds of many.
The younger generations may just be convinced there really was life before them!

164

Printed in the United Kingdom by
Lightning Source UK Ltd., Milton Keynes
139740UK00001B/174/P